CAPTAIN W. E. JOHNS

BIGGLES'
SPECIAL CASE

KNIGHT BOOKS
the paperback division of Brockhampton Press

ISBN 0 340 19087 6

This edition first published 1975 by Knight, the paperback
division of Brockhampton Press, Leicester.
First published in 1963 by Brockhampton Press Ltd

Text copyright © 1963 Capt. W. E. Johns

Printed and bound in Great Britain
by Cox & Wyman Ltd, London, Reading and Fakenham

This book is sold subject to the condition that it shall not
by way of trade or otherwise be lent, re-sold, hired out or
otherwise circulated without the publisher's prior consent
in any form of binding or cover other than that in which
this is published and without a similar condition including
this condition being imposed on the subsequent purchaser.

BIGGLES' SPECIAL CASE

The Air Commodore admitted to Biggles
that there was more to this mission to some
archaeological ruins in the Middle East than
he could explain. But it wasn't until Biggles
had been bombarded by jet fighters,
grounded by a sand-storm and involved in a
desert gun battle that he realised just what
was at stake.

CONTENTS

1	The Air Commodore sets the scene	7
2	An unwelcome guest	20
3	The ruins of Quarda	31
4	Trouble brewing	43
5	The enemy strikes	57
6	Questions without answers	69
7	Nature takes a hand	82
8	Rasal al Sharab	93
9	The truth comes out	106
10	Zorlan makes an offer	121
11	Biggles gets tough	132
12	The battle of Quarda	141
13	How it all ended	154

CHAPTER 1

THE AIR COMMODORE SETS THE SCENE

'COME in, Bigglesworth. I want to speak to you and what I have to say will take a little time. Bring your chair round to this side of the desk so that you can follow me on the map when I refer to it.' As he spoke Air Commodore Raymond, head of the Special Air police, moved his cigarette box and ashtray to where they could more easily be reached.

As Biggles settled in his chair he took a sidelong glance at his chief, knowing that he only spoke like this when something serious was in the air. He also looked at the map which, its corners held down by paper-weights, covered most of the top of the desk. He recognised Asia Minor. 'Right you are, sir, I'm ready,' he announced.

The Air Commodore spoke quietly. 'I'm going to ask you to undertake what might well turn out to be the most important mission of your career. If all goes well it could resolve itself into a perfectly simple operation involving nothing more difficult than a cross-country flight with some delicate navigation: but on the other hand, I must in fairness warn you that if things did not go according to plan you would almost certainly find yourself in an extremely difficult position. Not that I expect any trouble.'

Biggles reached for a cigarette, smiling sadly. 'It isn't what one expects on these jobs; it's what you don't expect that puts sand in the gear-box.'

The Air Commodore ignored the remark. 'I may as well tell you at once that should things go wrong there would be nothing I could do about it.'

'In plain English, the government would deny all knowledge of me and what I was doing, or was accused of doing.'

'Put it that way if you like.'

'I'm old enough to face facts. I never did like politics.'

'I haven't said anything about politics.'

'I can smell 'em a long way off.'

'Unfortunately it seems the world can't get along without them. But let us not waste time arguing about that,' continued the Air Commodore. 'A great deal of trouble has been devoted to the preparations for what I am going to ask you to do. Plans are not cut and dried down to the last detail and they are as perfect as it is humanly possible to make them.'

'That's something, anyway,' conceded Biggles. 'Suppose you give me a rough outline of the job. We can discuss the finer points later.'

'Very well. The operation consists of flying an aircraft, with a very special passenger, to a rather unusual objective in the Middle East. After what we may hope will be only a brief wait there – a matter of a few hours – the machine will probably have to go on to a second objective, taking the same passenger. From there, depending on what happens, and this I cannot predict with confidence, the aircraft will either return to the first objective or make the best of its way home. In this the decision will be made by your passenger.'

'One passenger only?'

'Just one.'

'May I know who he is?'

'No. As far as you are concerned he will be Professor Zorlan, of the British-Asian Archaeological Society.'

'Zorlan?' mused Biggles. 'Queer name. What colour is this gentleman, black or white?'

'Neither.' The Air Commodore offered a ghost of a smile. 'Let us say grey, with a touch of brown.' He became serious. 'Never mind his name or nationality. I can tell you this. Your passenger is in fact a scholar of repute with a remarkable knowledge of oriental languages and customs. He is also a practical archaeologist with experiences of the countries you will be visiting. That is as much as you need to know about him. I myself know little more. It is unlikely that you will have with him more personal contact than is absolutely necessary. Apart from the actual flying there will be nothing for you to do. Your passenger will attend to everything else.'

Biggles looked suspicious. 'Before we go any further, is this trip taking us the wrong side of the Iron Curtain?'

'No.'

'Thank goodness for that.'

'I should perhaps have added, not while you keep on your course. You won't be far away from it, so be careful.'

'You can rely on that,' returned Biggles grimly.

'Now for your own identity,' continued the Air Commodore. 'You can travel under your own name, but you will leave at home anything that might connect you with the police, or any British government department. For the time being you will be a civil pilot flying for an air charter company named Planet Transport Ltd. You have been ordered by the company to fly Professor Zorlan to his destination, wait for him and return. Forget everything else. Special identity papers in that capacity are being prepared for you.'

Biggles nodded. 'That's clear enough. Do I go on this jaunt alone?'

'No. As a precautionary measure you will take a spare pilot with you. By that I mean one who will sit beside you able to take over in an emergency. I leave it to you to decide which member of your staff occupies that position.'

Biggles frowned. 'You talk as if something could happen to me. What *could* happen to me? Is there any possibility of the aircraft coming under fire?'

The Air Commodore hesitated. 'That's a leading question. While you keep on course I can't see why it should. You won't be flying over hostile country, although you know as well as I do that any odd Arab may have a poop at an aeroplane just for the hell of it. The only honest answer I can give you is, on an outlandish operation of this sort anything might happen. Much is bound to depend on our security arrangements, and they've been kept as tight as a limpet on a rock.'

'What you mean is, there are people who would object to this programme and would go to any lengths to prevent it from being successful.'

'That's about the size of it.'

'In that case would you advise us to carry firearms – for self-defence only, of course.'

'You must please yourself about that, but I must point out that if you ran into trouble, and were found to be carrying weapons, you would be hard put to reconcile them with the avowed purpose of your flight.'

'Yes, I see that. Carry on, sir.'

'About your crew. If you would care to take an extra hand with you, you may. He would have to occupy a seat in the cabin with the passenger, under the pretence of being his assistant, or secretary. There will be plenty of room. I shall leave this to you.'

'And the purpose of this flight?'

'Officially it is to enable your passenger to revisit certain ruins, on the site of your first objective, to check up on something that was overlooked on the occasion of a previous visit. He has been there before. He was a member of the party which in 1960, by permission, spent a month doing some preliminary work preparatory to organising a full scale dig, as it is called, for information the ground might yield about the original inhabitants. This part of the world was the cradle of civilisation, and the place we're talking about was a flourishing town in the year 2000 B.C., perhaps earlier.'

'Very interesting for those who like pottering with old pots, but I'm more interested in the aircraft. I shall want something reliable.'

'That's all been attended to. It has been arranged for you to take over one of the new eight-seater jobs now coming off the production line. It was designed for feeder lines to work in conjunction with the main trunk routes.'

'I've seen photographs of the machine, but of course I've never flown one. It looks a nice job.'

'It should give you everything you want in the way of

speed and endurance range. It can climb with full load, on one engine if necessary. You'll be flying over rough country, so you'll have an ample margin for safety in the unlikely event of engine failure. You'd better have a trial run in the Merlin to get the feel of it. You have a few days to spare. Now let's have a look at the map to see exactly where you're going. The route has been prepared.' The Air Commodore picked up the pencil and leaned forward over the map, guiding the point to illustrate his words.

'You'll pick up Professor Zorlan at Gatwick on a day and at a time yet to be fixed. You will fly non-stop to Rome. There you will refuel. You will then proceed, again non-stop, to Istanbul, taking care to keep clear of Albania, which as you know is a Communist dictatorship. At Istanbul you will of course have to report your arrival in Turkey. From there a short run of two hundred miles will take you to Ankara, where your passenger will leave you for a short while and in any case you will have to stay the night. A regular air service operates over this part of the route, so you should have no difficulties.'

'You're sure the Turkish authorities will raise no objection?'

'They shouldn't. Your papers will be in order and permission of the Turkish Government, through their London office, has been obtained for you to fly over their territory to the objective; the purpose being, as I have already said, to enable Professor Zorlan to make a fresh survey of some ruins I will presently describe. The Turkish Archaeological Society is itself interested in these ancient remains and very obligingly co-operated with the last expedition. That was not an airborne operation. Trucks were used to take the men and equipment to the site.'

'Does this mean there will be digging?'

'No. Anyway, not on this occasion. Naturally, having realised the value of prehistoric monuments, no government today will allow excavating without supervision. It takes over, quite properly, anything that is found. But as I have said, so far all should be plain sailing. It is from now on that you might possibly run into – well, if not trouble, complications.'

'Can you be a little more specific? What sort of trouble could there be?'

The Air Commodore shrugged. 'You know how it is. Ankara, like every other city in a country that happens to occupy a strategical position, will have its share of spies, and there is always a chance that one might take an interest in an aircraft showing British registration markings.'

Biggles nodded assent. 'So I fly on over Turkish territory?'

'Not altogether. That, I'm afraid, is a matter of argument. You'll understand what I mean by that in a moment. At all events, both in Ankara and beyond, you would be well advised to take particular note of anything unusual, both on the ground and in the air.'

'I certainly will.' Biggles was vehement.

The Air Commodore went on, using his pencil. 'When you leave Ankara you will take up a course slightly south of east for a run of about four hundred miles when you will come to an area just about as far out of the civilised world as you could find today. You will be out in the blue over the hills and deserts named in the Old Testament of the Bible, actually the land where the earliest civilisations began. On your way you may see a few desert bus routes or caravan trails, but you won't find any servicing facilities. Your objective is an ancient settlement, now in ruins, named Quarda. It used to be an oasis, but apparently the water dried up. Here it is.' The Air Commodore marked the spot with his pencil. 'You have two good landmarks, the first a twin peak named Kaelbeg Dagh, at the foot of which there is a small lake of brackish water called Ozro Shah. Here we are. You're still with me?'

Biggles nodded.

'Good. There are reasons to believe that Quarda is the site of one of the oldest human dwelling-places on the face of the earth. It goes back at least to the year 4000 B.C. It has only recently been located. We know the ancient Greeks reached it for they built a temple there. Most of it is now flat, apparently having been shaken down by an earthquake at some time. However, three Ionic columns are still standing and these with a few palm trees should pin-point your actual objective. Professor Zorlan will identify the place, anyhow, having been there. He is an authority on early civilisations.'

'Does anyone live there now?'

'No. A passing Arab may call for some dates, should there be any, or to see if there is any water in the old well; that's about all.'

'And this place is actually in Turkey?' queried Biggles.

'No, it is not, and this is where we hit the first snag. It is in the sheikhdom of Zarat, an area of land to which Turkey, Armenia and Kurdistan all lay claim. I imagine the only reason why they haven't gone to war over it is because the whole area is arid and useless for any practical purpose. But in these days when every upstart dictator is on the grab to enhance his reputation, it can only be a matter of time before the question boils up again to start an international rumpus.'

'You call this territory a sheikhdom. Is there a ruling sheikh?'

'Yes, but I'm happy to tell you there will not be any trouble from him. He knows what is intended. He lives in a mud-brick palace in his capital, a small place called Zarana, about thirty miles from the ruins of Quarda, content while things are quiet to let the rest of the world go by. His chief activity is breeding horses and camels, of which he and his forebears have developed fine strains. He also breeds hawks for hunting gazelle. He merely wants things to stay as they are; but with Armenia, which is in the Soviet Republic, on his doorstep, he must realise that his position is far from secure. It's unlikely that you'll see him. The ruins are your primary concern.'

'How about landing conditions?'

'You needn't worry about that. For many miles around, apart from the mountain I mentioned, the terrain is as flat as an ironing board, nothing but *sabkha* which, as you know, is a sort of hard packed sandy gravel.'

Biggles reached for another cigarette. 'So I fly to Quarda, land my passenger near the ruins – and then what?'

'You simply wait for him to return from the ruins, where he has an appointment. He shouldn't be away long.'

'Then we return home?'

'Not necessarily. That would mean that the mission

had failed. Zorlan will tell you what to do. It is hoped that he will ask you to take him on to Rasal al Sharab.'

Biggles frowned. 'Where the devil's that? I've been around, but you're trotting out some names I've never heard of.'

'Few people have.' The Air Commodore again used his pencil. 'Rasal al Sharab is a small sultanate no great distance south, lying between the borders of Iraq and Iran. For the sake of peace and quiet it's described officially as neutral territory. Again it's a pretty remote corner, mostly desert and a few scattered oases, with here and there a collection of mud-brick dwellings which Arabs would call towns. You're not likely to have any trouble with Iran unless you cross the frontier, but I wouldn't be too sure of Iraq as things are at present.'

'Do I understand the people of Rasal al Sharab are Arabs?'

'No. They're a race of their own. They speak a Persian dialect and mind their own business, which consists chiefly of raising goats and harvesting a few meagre agricultural products. Like the people of Zarat they ask nothing more than to be left alone, but unfortunately for them their position is as insecure as Zarat, in that sooner of later someone will try to swallow them. Again you should have no difficulty in getting down. All you will have to do is wait while your passenger makes a call on the Sultan.'

'And then?'

'He'll tell you what to do.'

Biggles tapped the ash off his cigarette. 'This all sounds a bit vague. What's the idea of making it an air operation?'

'Firstly, speed. Secondly, you couldn't run an overland expedition without a lot of people knowing about it and they would demand to be told why.'

'I see. It looks as if we might be in the middle of nowhere for some days. What do we use for food? I'm nothing for a diet of dates and dried figs.'

'You'll have whatever you care to take with you. There's plenty of accommodation. The aircraft is equipped with a small kitchen and even a refrigerator. It's the last word in air transportation.'

'Fair enough.' Biggles looked pensive.

The Air Commodore turned to him. 'What's on your mind?'

'You won't think me inquisitive if I wonder what all this is about, that's all,' returned Biggles casually. 'Would I be right in supposing it's an attempt to bring together two little inoffensive states, for their mutual benefit and possibly protection?'

'That would give them a greater importance,' admitted the Air Commodore.

'And there are some people who wouldn't approve of this hook-up.'

The Air Commodore sighed. 'You're too smart. Does it matter?'

'Where my life's concerned everything matters. I have only one and I'd prefer to hang on to it as long as possible. Naturally, I like to know what risks I'm taking before I start, instead of bumping into them half-way. Am I right in thinking that if certain people knew about this jaunt they'd try to push a spoke through the wheel?'

'Frankly, yes.'

'Ah! I'm beginning to get the drift. When is this enterprise due to take off?'

'Not for a few days. I'll let you know. It is being arranged so that there should be no waiting by either side at the two objectives. I think that's as much as you need know.'

'Tell me this, sir,' requested Biggles. 'Does Turkey know what's in the wind?'

'The only answer I can give to that is, Turkey as a friendly country has raised no objection to Professor Zorlan making a flying trip to the ruins of Quarda. On no account may she be embarrassed. Having a frontier with Soviet Russia, one could hardly expect her to risk serious diplomatic trouble by agreeing openly to outside interference within her boundaries. The day of small defenceless nations is about finished and sooner or later the two little states with which we are concerned will disappear. Indeed, that could happen at any time. Even if Zarat and Rasal al Sharab had a mutual assistance pact it would be futile for them to attempt to resist aggression, but together they'd have a better chance of calling the attention of the United Nations to their plight if they were overrun.'

Biggles stubbed his cigarette. 'Yes, I see that.'

'But my advice to you is to know as little as possible about the political angle and forget what has been hinted at here. The less you know the less you would be able to reveal if you were questioned. Stick to your cover story about being nothing more than a civil pilot engaged to fly Professor Zorlan to the ruins of Quarda for a brief archaeological survey prior to the resumption of digging when weather conditions permit.'

'What about the Professor?'

'He will tell the same story and you can rely on him to play up to it. The fact that he is an archaeologist, who has already been to the ruins, will support him.'

'This previous digging. Was that kept secret?'

'No. It was all open and above board and the results were published in the Press. The excavating was done by native labour, so there was no question of keeping it under the hat. There was no need.'

'And there was no trouble on that occasion?'

'None whatever. But I must admit that since that time there has been a change in the general political situation. Should the digging be resumed, as it may be, Russia might protest that her frontier was being threatened. Quite absurd, of course, considering that the total population of Zarat is under three thousand. But as you know, the Communist countries see, or pretend to see, a threat in everything, and in consequence are touchy even on the most trifling matters. Any more questions?'

'I can't think of any at the moment,' replied Biggles after a pause. 'I may think of something later when I've digested what you've told me. I shall probably take Lissie as spare pilot and put Ginger in the cabin with the passenger. That would leave Algy to take care of anything that might turn up while I'm away.'

'As you wish.'

'Shall I meet Professor Zorlan before we start?'

'It's unlikely. There's no reason why you should. You'll hardly come in contact with him if everything goes as planned. He'll simply be your employer and you'll take orders from him.'

Biggles got up. 'Very well, sir. I'll go and have a look at the aircraft.'

CHAPTER 2

AN UNWELCOME GUEST

A FORTNIGHT after Biggles' conversation with the Air Commodore he stood, with Bertie and Ginger, on the airport at Ankara awaiting the arrival of their passenger from the hotel where he had spent the night. After an uneventful run from Gatwick they themselves had slept in a small hotel nearer the aerodrome. So far everything had gone smoothly, and the Merlin, with its tanks full, was now all set to continue its journey.

Biggles was happy about its performance which was all that had been claimed for it. It was a pleasure to fly, and would, like most modern commercial aircraft, practically fly itself. A new type, only just coming into production, it was equipped with all the latest devices for safety, efficiency and comfort. As he remarked, no pilot could ask for more. The only fault Bertie could find was that a chef had not been provided to operate in the kitchenette and serve iced drinks as required. This, no doubt, was prompted by the fact that the weather was extremely hot.

No changes had been made in the original arrangement. Bertie, as co-pilot, occupied the seat beside

Biggles, and Ginger sat in the cabin from which a small door, with a glass panel, gave access to the cockpit. His companion had hardly spoken a word and passed the time reading.

In one respect Biggles had not accepted the Air Commodore's advice. This was in the matter of firearms. Aware of the disadvantage of being without any means of defence should they run into active opposition, he had been to some pains to hide inside his cushioned seat two small loaded pocket automatics. It was true that the Air Commodore had asserted fairly confidently that the project was not likely to encounter interference; but Biggles, who still did not know the true purpose of his passenger in visiting the ruins of Quarda (he was not deceived by the official reason), preferred not to find himself helpless in an emergency. In this he was not thinking of the airports at which they would be calling, but of what might happen on the ground in the wild region of his objective. So he resolved to take a chance and risk the guns being found *en route* should the aircraft be searched. In that event he thought they would simply be taken away from him. However, that had not happened, so the chance had come off.

Professor Zorlan had arrived at Gatwick punctually. This was the first time any of the crew had seen him. His greeting was a curt nod, which was taken to mean that from the outset he wanted it to be known that he was in charge and had no time to waste on casual conversation. As this was understandable his off-hand attitude was accepted without resentment.

Aside from his manner, his appearance was in accord with his part of playing the 'mystery man'. He was about forty years of age, of medium height and build, too swarthy to be of pure European birth, and wore a small, pointed, well-trimmed black beard. His hair, too, was black, and receded slightly from his forehead. Horn-rimmed glasses covered dark eyes that had a disconcerting, calculating quality of penetration, as if trying to read the thoughts of anyone on whom they were turned. His nose was thin but well shaped over lips a trifle too full by European standards. Taken all in all he was a good-looking man, and there was in the way he carried himself the confidence of one accustomed to giving, not receiving, orders. From head to foot, everything he wore, the standard attire of a London business man, was of top quality and immaculate. He brought with him a light-weight suitcase and a leather portfolio. Later it transpired that he spoke English fluently without a trace of accent.

Biggles, who from experience had become a fair judge of character, didn't know what to make of him. He was content, as indeed he had to be, to accept him at the face value provided by the Air Commodore. As to the man's real nationality, his religion, politics, or anything else, as he said to the others with a shrug, it was anyone's guess. As far as they were concerned it was of no importance, anyway. If the Higher Authority at home was satisfied who were they to criticise?

Some care had been given to the provision of the food that would be required, and in this matter, having plenty of accommodation and an ice-box, they could afford to extend themselves, instead of being, as they usually were on long trips, confined to bare necessities. Stores included a considerable quantity of soda-water, which would, it was hoped, remove the risk of having to drink water that might be contaminated – as desert water-holes so often are.

Biggles looked at his watch. 'Time we were off,' he observed. 'I hope the Professor isn't going to be late. I'd like to have most of the run behind us before the sun gets really cracking. It's going to be a scorcher presently.'

'What does this chap want?' queried Ginger. 'He's coming this way as if he intends to speak to us.'

His eyes were on a plump, smartly dressed man who, carrying an expensive-looking suitcase, was making his way towards them. He wore a white flannel suit, white shoes and a panama hat. A red tie made a conspicuous spot of colour against a white shirt. His age could have been anything between forty and fifty. For the rest he was a type common in the Eastern Mediterranean. His skin was dusky rather than dark, with a peculiar olive pallor. A large moustache was worn brushed up at the ends. His eyes were large, black and heavy – what is sometimes described as 'liquid'. His movements were slow and languid, like those of a well-fed house cat just awakened from sleep.

'The lad fancies himself a bit,' remarked Bertie. 'It's my guess he's a Turkish official.'

'Considering where we are there would be nothing surprising in that,' returned Biggles casually. 'Probably something to do with the airport.'

The object of their conjectures, smiling amiably, came straight up to them. Putting his case on the ground he looked at Biggles and offered his hand. 'Captain Bigglesworth?' he queried.

'That's my name,' agreed Biggles, shaking hands without enthusiasm. 'Can I do something for you?'

'No, thank you. Not for the moment,' was the reply, given pleasantly, in good English. Smiling again the man went on: 'I thought I would come in good time to introduce myself. Colonel Osman Alfondari, at your service. I see Professor Zorlan has not yet arrived.'

Biggles was looking puzzled. 'What service for me have you in mind, Colonel?'

'I have the honour, under orders of my government, to be your escort.'

Biggles stared. 'My *escort*! For what?'

'I shall see that no harm comes to you.'

'Surely this is unnecessary? What harm could come to us?'

'One never knows. Some of the people towards our eastern and southern frontiers are little better than barbarians: and they are notorious thieves.'

'We can take care of ourselves.'

'We could not permit an accident to happen.'

'Are you telling me that you are going to *fly* with us?'

'But of course. How else could I do my duty?'

For a few seconds Biggles was speechless. 'I've heard nothing about such an arrangement.'

'But surely you were told that we always provide an escort for strangers going into the interior?'

'This is the first I've heard about it. I haven't made provision for an extra passenger.'

Still smiling blandly the other brushed the objection aside. 'Oh come, my dear Captain, you have ample room for more passengers. I shall not take up much space and promise not to interfere in any way.'

Biggles thought for a moment. 'Tell me this, Colonel.

Suppose we did have a little trouble, what could you do that we could not do?'

'Nobody would dare to argue with me for fear of the consequences.'

Biggles' eyes went beyond the speaker to where Professor Zorlan, a boy following carrying his luggage, was walking towards them. 'Excuse me a minute,' he said, and went forward to meet him.

When they met he asked bluntly: 'Do you know anything about an escort being briefed to come with us?'

The Professor stopped. A frown creased his forehead. 'An escort! I know nothing about it. I have just left a Turkish Government official and he did not mention it.'

'If this is a regular procedure he may have assumed you would know about it.'

'That could be so.'

Biggles went on. 'Well, there's a fellow here calling himself Colonel Osman Alfondari who says he's been detailed to accompany us on the next stage of our journey. His purpose, he informs me, is to see that we do not come to any harm. Personally, I think it's more likely that he intends to see what we're up to.'

'Does he know where we're going?'

'He hasn't said so in so many words. I haven't asked him. But he obviously knows, or at any rate assumes, that we shall be flying east from here. Doesn't it strike you as odd that the Turkish Government did not inform you of the condition under which you would be allowed to enter the country?'

'The arrangements were made at the London embassy. They may not have known of it.'

'Well, we have now been told. If the Turkish officials

know where we are going it's reasonable to suppose that our escort would be told. That leaves me wondering how many other people know about it.'

'This is very difficult.' Still frowning the Professor fingered his beard thoughtfully. 'I was not prepared for anything of the sort. How can we refuse to take this officer without causing trouble? It would be thought we had something to hide.'

'Haven't we?'

The Professor gave Biggles a quick glance. He was looking more and more perturbed. Ignoring the question he said: 'I'm afraid we shall have to take him with us. To refuse might result in us being turned back. My purpose is to enter the ruins of Quarda. When I leave you to do that, you having landed on the open ground, this man must on no account be allowed to follow me.'

'Suppose he insists? How am I to prevent it?'

'Use your discretion.'

'How could that stop him should he make up his mind to go with you?'

'I leave that to you.'

Biggles looked hard at the Professor's face. 'Are you suggesting that I use *force*?'

'If necessary. I repeat, on no account must he be allowed to see what I am doing. That could be fatal and perhaps have tremendous consequences.'

'How far am I to carry force?'

'As far as is necessary.'

'But how shall we explain our behaviour when we arrive back here and he accuses us of preventing him from carrying out his duties?'

'That need not arise.'

'But he'd be certain to complain.'

'Not necessarily.'

'I don't understand.'

'He need not return with us.'

Biggles looked startled. 'Are you suggesting that if we have trouble with him we should leave him behind?'

'It would be better to dispose of him entirely.'

'You mean – *kill* him?'

'That would settle any argument.'

'Good grief!' Biggles was genuinely shocked. For the first time he caught a glimpse of the ruthless nature of his passenger. 'Let's get this clear,' he said grimly. 'I'm not shooting an unarmed man.'

'He will be armed.'

'How do you know?'

'Of what use would be an escort without a weapon? What's the matter with you? You must have known before we started that you were engaged in an operation of major diplomatic importance.'

'I don't care how important it is, I'm having nothing to do with murder,' said Biggles shortly. 'You've got the wrong man.'

'It may never arise.' Speaking quietly and dispassionately the Professor went on. 'If we return to Ankara we can say he was shot by a native sniper. Such accidents are not uncommon in this part of the world.'

'You say *if* we return to Ankara as if there was a doubt about it.'

'We are not obliged to return here, although I would prefer to do so in order to get proper clearance papers. When my work is concluded we can leave the country by any route we wish and explain the reason later. When you land it will not for obvious reasons be among the actual ruins. It will be on the open *sabkha* as near as possible. There I shall leave you to await my return. Should this man try to follow me into the ruins he must be stopped. That is an order.'

'Very well; but somebody is going to take a dim view of it if we lay hands on this Colonel fellow.'

'I think you have overlooked a certain factor. Assuming he is a Turk, he will not, at the ruins, be on his own soil. He will be in Zarat, a very different matter, without authority. Unless he knows our destination and has provided himself with the necessary documents he will have no right to be there at all. The Sheikh, with justification, could complain. Indeed, he might take the law into his own hands.'

'Turkey has a claim to the territory.'

'A claim is one thing and possession is another. A claim would at once be disputed by other claimants. As things are, it is in the interest of Turkey that the present position should continue.'

Biggles shook his head. 'I don't like it.'

'Whether you like it or not there can be no withdrawal now. Things have gone too far.' The Professor spoke coldly. 'I don't want this man with us any more than you do; but this is not the place to cause trouble, which could easily result in the cancellation of our permits.'

'Yes, I realise that,' agreed Biggles.

'Then we have no alternative than to take this man with us. We can deal later with problems his presence might incur. I will speak to him in the hope of finding out how much he knows.'

'If he knows no more than I do he knows damn little,' said Biggles, bitterly.

'Do not mention our destination unless he does.' Professor Zorlan walked on towards where the man concerned was chatting cheerfully with Bertie and Ginger.

'Don't be longer than is necessary,' requested Biggles. 'We're behind schedule already.'

'The people who once conquered this land had a saying: "It is sometimes a good thing to hurry slowly",' replied the Professor, smoothly.

'I was thinking of the heat. I can stand it if you can.'

They joined the others. The Professor spoke to the escort. 'I understand you are to accompany us,' he said in a voice that indicated neither approval nor disapproval.

'Those are my orders,' was the reply.

'You know where we are going?'

'Of course.'

'As we may be gone for a few days I trust you have provided yourself with what you will require in the way of food and drink. Knowing nothing of this stipulation we catered only for ourselves.'

'I can manage.'

Professor Zorlan then spoke in a language Biggles did not understand, but presumed it to be Turkish. Colonel Alfondari answered in what apparently was the same tongue. It seemed to satisfy the Professor, who speaking again in English, concluded with: 'Very well. Then we might as well proceed.' He moved towards the open door of the aircraft.

Biggles hung back, touching Ginger on the arm. 'This

business is beginning to stink,' he said softly. 'Keep a close eye on our new travelling companion for anything he might do that doesn't line up with what he's supposed to be.'

Ginger raised his eyebrows. 'Why? Don't you trust him?'

'He smiles too much, and that, on a job like this, looks false. Moreover, he strikes me as being a little too cock-sure of himself.'

'Then why not challenge him?'

'Zorlan is against it. He says if we were wrong it could start a fuss which might end with us being told to go home. He could be right. He's a queer type, too – but I'll tell you more about that later.'

'So you're expecting trouble?'

'I detect an atmosphere which has nothing to do with the weather.'

No more was said. Everyone took his place in the aircraft. The engines were started. Biggles gave them a minute or two, and with his eyes on the instrument panel ran them up. Satisfied he taxied out, and receiving permission from the control officer, took off.

CHAPTER 3

THE RUINS OF QUARDA

At a height of six thousand feet the Merlin bored along its calculated course, thrusting the overheated air behind it at a speed of a little under 400 m.p.h. A higher altitude would have been more comfortable, for the air, lashed by the tireless sun, was turbulent, and the aircraft for all its speed sometimes rose and fell on an invisible swell; but more height would have made it difficult to pick out the meagre landmarks Biggles had noted on the map.

The sky was not the rich cornflower blue of the humid tropics but a dome that had the hard brightness of burnished steel. Under it the foreground shimmered. The horizon, marked by a ragged line of mountains, was blurred by heat-haze. Conspicuous far away to the north-east rose the 16,000 foot peak of Mount Ararat, the traditional resting-place of Noah's Ark. The River Halys, the ancient dividing line between East and West, had already drifted away astern.

Ahead, the hinterland of Eastern Anatolia turned an ugly face to the pitiless heavens, reflecting a glare which worried the eyes and distorted such features of the landscape as were presented to it.

For the most part the earth was the colour of putty. It

looked tired, worn out, its surface cracked by innumerable quakes and tremors, wrinkled and dotted with excrescences like the skin of an old toad. Hills, like warts, rose starkly from the plain, sometimes isolated, sometimes in groups. Nowhere was there rest for the eyes, no colour to break the monotony; nor would there be until the spring rains came to refresh for a little while the parched and arid soil. Across the wilderness gaunt grey hills and rock formations cast patterns of blue-black shadows. There was still an occasional village, whitened by distance and looking like a handful of toy bricks dropped by a careless child, linked by a network of wandering trails. Of human activity there was no sign. Animals were represented by small herds of what were probably sheep or goats, usually not far away from a group of palms that may have clustered round a waterhole. For the rest, there were merely areas of that hardy plant of desert countries, the camel-thorn. Everywhere lay boulders exposed by erosion.

Bertie, looking down on this inhospitable scene through his side window, found it hard to believe that this was where civilisation began; where civilisations had come, had had their day and vanished long before such words as Rome and Europe had been coined; the land that had seen and made more history than any other in the world. Here had been fought the terrible prehistoric wars of extermination described in the Old Testament of the Bible. Here had flourished the great Hittite Empire. The dreaded Assyrians. The Sumerians had dominated it for fifteen hundred years, during which period they had invented the first known system of writing. Here had marched the hosts of the Medes and Persians; Alexander the Great and his conquering

Greeks, Xenophon and his gallant Ten Thousand, Roman Legions . . . all had come and gone long before Christ was born, leaving little to mark their passage through Time. No wonder this part of the earth's surface was called The Old World.

Biggles had told Bertie of his conversation with Professor Zorlan about Colonel Alfondari. 'We'd better be prepared for trouble,' he said gloomily. 'Actually, I don't see why there should be any as long as Alfondari will stay with the machine and not try to poke his nose into the ruins while Zorlan is there. If that should happen it will be Zorlan we shall have to keep under control. I can't make him out, and that's a fact. He looks all right and I feel he must be all right, but the way he talked calmly of bumping off Alfondari if he gets in the way made me go cold. I can tell you this: he's not made of ordinary flesh and blood. He's got acid in his veins and a lump of granite where his heart should be. He's ruthless, a bit too ruthless for my liking, and so determined to let nothing stand in his way that I begin to wonder what he's getting out of it.'

'Maybe that's why he was chosen for the job.'

'Could be. But I'd rather work with somebody human.'

'You can bet Alfondari will want to see what's going on,' asserted Bertie. 'I wonder if he carries a gun and if he'd dare to use it if it came to a show-down.'

'Zorlan thinks he's certain to have a gun in his pocket, taking the view that he'd be no use as an escort without a weapon. We couldn't very well ask him. No doubt we shall know about that soon enough. To be on the safe side we might as well have ours on us. There's no longer any risk of them being found. You know where they are. Get them out while I have a look behind.'

While Bertie was collecting the automatics Biggles snatched a glance through the glass panel in the bulk-head door. Zorlan was reading. Alfondari was looking down from one window and Ginger from another. No one was talking.

Bertie, having got the pistols, took a look. 'A nice cheerful party I must say,' he observed. 'Anyone would think we were on our way to a funeral.'

'We might be. The thing is to take care it isn't ours,' returned Biggles dryly.

'You're a nice cheerful Jonah,' growled Bertie.

'I only hope Zorlan doesn't include air pilotage with his other accomplishments.'

'What do you mean by that?'

'Zorlan has no more love for us than he has for Alfondari. We're nothing to him. He doesn't even know us. Why should he care two hoots about what happens to us? If he's prepared to come back without Alfondari he might be equally prepared to come back without us – that is, if he can manage the aircraft. Maybe I'm wrong. I may be doing him an injustice. I doubt if we'd ever get to know him, but of this I am sure. He's a man who will stop at nothing to get what he wants. I'm not squeamish, but as I said just now, the way he talked of getting rid of Alfondari, if he got in the way, shook me. When a man can talk casually of killing another, no matter who he may be, he's capable of anything.'

'He might have been talking big – bluffing. We've met people like that.'

Biggles shook his head. 'He's no bluffer. Anyway, I hope I shall never have to put it to the test.'

'You don't trust him?'

'I'd prefer to reserve my opinion until we've seen more of him.'

'I wonder who he really is and what he hopes to get out of this.'

'There wouldn't be any point in asking him. It would be easier to open an oyster with a toothpick than get to the inside of him. Still, there may be reasons for that. Our trouble is we don't really know what we're doing.'

'Zorlan knows what *he's* doing.'

'I don't doubt that. The Air Commodore may have known more than he told me. If so he must have been sworn to silence or he wouldn't have let us fly blind into this sort of country. I fancy he had a feeling that we might run into trouble, but he may not have known where it would come from. But why talk about it? We're in it up to the neck. The thing will have to work itself out and that shouldn't take long now. Biggles looked at the watch on the instrument panel. 'According to my E.T.A. we must be getting close.'

Shortly after this, gazing ahead, he altered course slightly. 'I can see what could be the twin peaks of Kaelbeg Dagh,' he observed. 'I can also see a hump that might be our objective.'

'Shall I tell Zorlan?'

'Not yet. He won't be able to see from where he's sitting. I'll drop off a little height as we get closer. The three columns should tell us if we're right. If we are it will be time enough to let the others know.'

'I think you're right,' said Bertie, frowning into the glare. 'I can't see any sign of a lake, though.'

'It will probably lie in a hollow. Or, of course, it may be dry.'

'What about the countries ahead of us, the mountains along the horizon?'

'According to my reckoning they should be Russian Armenia, and a bit more to starboard, Kurdistan. I imagine we wouldn't be welcome in either.'

The aircraft, losing height, was now fast approaching an extensive mound of wind-blown sand, nearly two hundred yards in diameter, which many centuries of time had heaped over what, from the projecting ruins, had in the antedeluvian period been a town. It rose like a boil on the flat face of the plain, a grim reminder of the end that awaits the works of men when the builders have had their day and gone. A few bedraggled palms, some leaning awry as if from utter weariness, their sun-dried fronds hanging uselessly like broken arms in the motionless air, clustered in groups or formed a frieze against the skyline.

Here and there a block of stone or the end of a broken column protruded from the tortured earth like tombs in an abandoned churchyard. Some trenches connecting three or four square-cut holes were obviously the work of recent excavators. But perhaps most important of all from the point of view of recognition, three Ionic columns, one still wearing its capital, stood erect as if to point accusing fingers at the heedless dome of heaven.

'This must be the place,' said Biggles to Bertie as, continuing to lose height, he began a circuit, the aircraft rocking in the turbulent thermals. 'Zorlan having been here before should recognise the place. When I've finished a circuit, so that we've had a clear view from all angles, you might ask him to confirm it.'

From a height of less than a hundred feet Biggles completed his inspection. There was not much to see.

The general outlines of the buildings could be traced, the old walls in one or two places rising several feet above the sand. They appeared not to have been shaken down by earthquakes, or deliberately broken down by conquering invaders, but had simply been silted up by sand carried on the prevailing wind. This was typical of many old towns and villages in the Middle East. That is to say, they were not built on a mound in the first place. The mound was formed and steadily grew higher partly from drifting sand and partly from household rubbish being dumped over the encircling wall built for defence.

'Have a word with Zorlan,' said Biggles. 'You can tell him there's nobody here. Had there been we would have seen horses or camels. At least, I can't imagine anyone walking here.'

Bertie went aft. 'This is it,' he confirmed on his return. 'Zorlan says it doesn't matter much where you land but get in as close as possible. By gosh! Someone, Alfondari I imagine, has filled the cabin with a nice old-fashioned oriental aroma.'

'Of what?'

'Garlic. The place stinks. Alfondari must chew the stuff raw.'

'Why not? It's said to be good for the stomach, and that isn't a modern idea.' Biggles smiled faintly. 'You may have forgotten that the children of Israel, on their march to the Promised Land, ratted on Moses when they ran out of onions and garlic.'

'Ha! Then I'm not surprised it took 'em forty years to get there.'

The subject was not pursued.

Said Biggles: 'I'll pull in under that group of palms on

the fringe of the hump. They should give us a little
shade. This sun would blister the hide of a rhino, never
mind an aircraft.' With that he brought the machine
round and put the wheels down gently on the hard-
packed *sabkha*, running on a little until he was within
the trellis-like shade pattern of the palms with the nose
of the aircraft pointing towards the open wilderness.

Everyone stepped out.

'Did you have to do all that manoeuvring after we
were on the ground?' inquired Zorlan irritably.

'I always like to park facing the way I'm going in case
I find it necessary to leave in a hurry,' returned Biggles
evenly.

Ginger explained later. It appeared that when the aircraft had run to its first stop Alfondari had stood up
preparatory to getting out. When it had gone on again,
turning in a tight circle to bring it into the position
Biggles wanted, he had lost his balance and fallen on the
Professor, much to his annoyance.

However, nothing more was said. The objective was
regarded in silence. It was as if everyone was waiting for
somebody to say something, or do something. Ginger
was conscious of a curious musty smell, as of things long
dead and forgotten. It was probably imagination, but it
seemed to carry with it a vague menace.

Biggles looked at Zorlan. 'Well, here we are,' he said
abruptly, as if he found the silence embarrassing. 'What
about it? What do you want us to do?'

For several long seconds Zorlan did not answer.
Looking somewhat incongruous with a portfolio in his
hand in such a place, he stood gazing at the mound as if
turning over a problem in his mind.

Ginger, too, had his first close look at the mound.

From ground level it was a good deal more broken than it had appeared from the air. Great blocks of stone lay about at all angles. Between them wind or storm-water had cut narrow gullies. Camel-thorn, sprouting like a grey beard that had never known a razor, flourished in patches. There was no sign of life, animal or insect. The only sound was the occasional harsh scrape of a bone-dry palm frond, as if someone was using a piece of sandpaper. There was one spot of colour. Bright red it hung on the topmost branch of a straggling bush. He recognised it as a ripe pomegranate.

Zorlan turned slowly, and beckoning to Biggles took him a little way on one side. 'Be very careful of this man Alfondari,' he said softly.

'You don't trust him?'

'I do not think he is Turkish. He speaks Turkish, but his accent is more that of a Turkoman from the Caspian coast. Do not lose sight of him.'

Biggles nodded.

'I shall take a walk into the ruins,' went on Zorlan. 'It is unlikely that I shall be away long.'

'Would you care to have something to eat, and a drink, before you go?'

'Not now. Later perhaps. I shall get a wider view from the top of the hill.'

Biggles shrugged. 'As you wish.'

Zorland turned away and started off up the mound, picking his route with care.

Biggles returned to the others to find that Alfondari had fetched his suitcase from the cabin. 'What are you going to do with that?' he asked, in genuine surprise.

'I may need it.'

'For what purpose?'

'If, as I suppose, we are to be here all night, I would rather sleep in the open than in the plane.'

'Nobody has said anything about staying here all night,' reminded Biggles.

'Very well. I will leave it here.' Alfondari stood the case at the base of a palm and started walking up the hill.

'Where are you going?' demanded Biggles sharply.

'To see the ruins. I have never seen them.'

'Stay here.'

Colonel Alfondari appeared not to have heard.

'Come back,' ordered Biggles, with iron in his voice.

Still Alfondari took no notice.

With his lips pressed in a hard line Biggles strode after him, put a hand on his shoulder and swung him round. 'You heard me,' he snapped. 'I said stay here.'

Alfondari shook off the restraining hand. 'You presume to give me orders?' he said haughtily.

'I do.'

'I am a Turkish officer.'

'You can be a Field Marshal for all I care. You're not in Turkey now.'

'What do you mean? I have my authority.'

'You have no authority here. This is Zarat. You know that as well as I do, so don't let's argue about it.'

Alfondari's dark eyes glowered. 'This will mean explanations when you return to Ankara.'

'You mean *if* we return to Ankara. Why are you so anxious to follow Professor Zorlan?'

'It is necessary to protect him.'

'From what? Against whom?'

'In country like this there is always danger. Raiders from Kurdistan may come, or Arabs.'

'You can leave me to deal with them. I am the captain of this aeroplane and I accept responsibility. Now come back and sit down, and let us have no more trouble.'

For some seconds Alfondari looked hard at Biggles' face. Then his manner suddenly changed. Once more he became the suave oriental. 'Very well. It shall be as you wish,' he said affably, with his slow smile.

Turning, he made his way back to the aircraft, collecting his suitcase on the way. From the door of the cabin he called: 'Do you mind if I give myself a drink?'

'Not at all. But don't take more than is necessary.'

Alfondari disappeared inside, taking his case with him. Biggles joined Bertie and Ginger who were sitting in the shade of the wing.

'What do you make of that?' asked Ginger.

'I don't know. Maybe he was only trying to throw his weight about. But now he's realised that doesn't cut any ice with me, we may not have any more bother with him. That doesn't mean I'd trust him farther than I could see him. Zorlan tells me he thinks he isn't a Turk.'

'Not a Turk!'

'He says he has the accent of a Turkoman from the Caspian.'

'And just what would that make him?'

'Probably a Caucasian from Georgia, which is behind the Iron Curtain. He could be a Persian.'

'That's a nice thought to go to bed with, I must say,' muttered Bertie. 'We should look a bunch of twits if it turned out we'd brought a Russian spy along with us.'

Biggles did not answer. He lit a cigarette and pushed the dead match viciously into the sand.

'He'd certainly made up his mind to follow Zorlan,' went on Bertie, breathing on his eyeglass and polishing it with his handkerchief.

'What puzzles me is why he was humping that suit-case up the hill with him,' said Ginger. 'Is there something in it he doesn't want us to see?'

Biggles looked up, a frown creasing his forehead. 'You may have hit on something there. Come to think of it he carried it as if it was a fair weight. I know he said at Ankara, when I objected to him coming with us on the grounds that we hadn't made provision for him, that he could supply his own food; but if that's the answer he must have brought enough to last a week or more.'

'Even so,' persisted Ginger, 'that wouldn't explain why he's determined, as he obviously is, not to let the case out of his sight.'

Biggles drew on his cigarette, looking at the aircraft. 'He's keeping quiet, anyhow. Maybe a bit too quiet. Ginger, go and see what he's doing.'

Ginger got up and walked across the soft sand to the cabin door.

The others, watching, saw him go in. In an instant he was standing in the doorway again. 'Biggles, come here,' he called cogently.

CHAPTER 4

TROUBLE BREWING

SUCH was the note of urgency in Ginger's voice that Biggles sprang to his feet and ran the short distance to the cabin door.

'Take a look at this,' requested Ginger, leading the way inside.

Biggles lost no time in so doing, and the reason for Ginger's concern was immediately apparent. No explanation was necessary.

Alfondari's case now lay open on a seat with the contents exposed. As Biggles' eyes fell on them the corners of his mouth came down in a spasm of anger. The case was a portable radio transmitter and Alfondari had begun to operate it.

In two swift paces Biggles had reached it and knocking away the operator's hands slammed it shut. 'What the hell do you think you're doing?' he rasped.

Alfondari looked up with a bland smile. 'I was merely about to report our safe arrival,' he answered smoothly.

'To whom?'

'My government, of course.'

'And which government is that?' rapped out Biggles cynically.

'Naturally, the Turkish Government.'

'Why didn't you tell me you had a radio transmitter?'

'I saw no reason to do so. What I carry is no concern of yours.'

'We'll see about that. You're not sending any messages from here, or anywhere else while you're with me.' So saying Biggles picked up the case and handed it to Ginger. 'Take that outside and dismantle it,' he ordered curtly.

'You have no right to interfere with me in the course of my duties,' cried Alfondari with a show of indignation.

'And you have no right to operate a radio outside Turkish territory,' snapped Biggles. 'I give the orders here. Any more tricks like this and I'll leave you in the desert to make your own way home.'

'But —'

'Don't argue with me. I said get outside – and stay where I can see you.'

Alfondari got up. He bowed, and putting on his slow, ever-ready smile, left the machine. He walked on languidly to a palm a short distance away and squatted on the tangle of small roots at the base.

Biggles watched him for a moment or two before rejoining the others. He was looking worried.

'That's settled that,' said Bertie, cheerfully.

'I'd like to think you're right,' answered Biggles, almost savagely.

'He won't send any more messages on this set, anyway,' announced Ginger as he scrambled the mechanism.

'I'm wondering how much information he was able to

get off before we stopped him,' muttered Biggles, sitting on the sand.

'It couldn't have been much, old boy; there wasn't time,' averred Bertie.

'Time enough, perhaps, to cause a packet of mischief. Zorlan was right. I'd rather have a rattlesnake around than this slick nosy-parker. With a snake you do at least know where you are.' Biggles looked calculatingly at Alfondari, still sitting with his back against the rough bole of the palm.

'Who do you suppose he was in touch with – or trying to make contact with?' asked Bertie seriously.

Biggles shook his head. 'How would I know? He may, as he claimed, have been doing nothing worse than report our arrival; but I have a feeling he was telling, or intended to tell, someone *where* we had landed. No doubt he was hoping, by following Zorlan, to say *why* we'd come here. He probably knows the official reason but obviously doesn't believe it. Don't forget that here we're uncomfortably close to more than one country that would resent our interference in the affairs of Zarat – if in fact that's why we're here. It wouldn't take a patrol long to get here to make things awkward for us – to say the least. A hostile aircraft could be over in a matter of minutes.'

'You mean, from the other side of the Iron Curtain?'

'From any of the countries that would like to grab Zarat. If one of them arrived here this could be a hot spot. One thing sticks out a mile. We can't afford to let this precious Colonel out of our sight for a moment.'

'Now we've taken his radio what could he do?' Ginger asked the question.

'He might sabotage the aircraft.'

Bertie scoffed at the idea. 'Oh, but look here, old boy. As he's a passenger in it he wouldn't be such an imbecile to do anything like that.'

'He might if it suited him to keep us grounded here until such time as pals of his came along to pick him up. What pains me is we shall have to share our food with him. Now we've seen the inside of his case it's certain he hasn't brought any with him. That makes him a liar, anyhow.'

'He must have known we'd find out,' put in Ginger.

'Not necessarily. It could be that he didn't reckon on being here very long.'

'What are we to deduce from that?'

'One answer could be that he has friends not far away. Talking of food, it's time we were having a snack. I was waiting for Zorlan. I wonder how long he's going to be.'

'He said he wouldn't be long.'

'I know that's what he *said*. It's a question of what he meant by not long. I fancy he was to meet somebody here. I didn't see anyone as we flew over before landing, and had anyone arrived since, we'd have heard him even if we didn't see him. I give it up. The whole business bristles with contradictions and the sooner we're finished with it the better.'

'Let's have a drink, anyway,' suggested Bertie.

'We might as well.'

They were moving towards the open door of the aircraft when Ginger observed: 'Here comes Zorlan now.'

They stopped and waited while the Professor, unsmiling, made his way down the rough slope of the mound, presently to join them.

'Everything all right?' inquired Biggles.

'No. The person I was to meet has not yet arrived. That is not to say he isn't coming. The meeting was arranged for today, but in such a place as this there is an excuse for unpunctuality. My man has some distance to travel.'

'I take it that means we shall have to wait?'

'Of course.' The Professor was looking at Alfondari, still squatting with his back to the palm. 'What's the matter with him?'

'I've had to take a strong line.'

'Indeed. For what reason?'

'In the first place he tried to follow you, and he got on the high horse when I made him come back. But there's more to it than that. His suitcase packed a portable radio transmitter. We only knew that when we caught him in the act of sending a signal. I put a stop to that and took the instrument away from him. It has been dismantled and is minus one or two vital components.'

For perhaps half a minute Zorlan looked Biggles in the face without speaking. Then, 'Is that so?' he breathed. 'For how long was he signalling before you stopped him?'

'Not long. Less than a minute, I think. He was sending in Morse, either in code or a language I couldn't read but as there was some repetition he may not have got beyond his call sign.'

'I sincerely hope you are right. Did you ask him what he was doing?'

'I did, without wasting words.'

'How did he explain his behaviour?'

'He made the obvious excuse that he was merely reporting our safe arrival to his headquarters.'

'Did you believe that?'

'No.'

'I warned you this man was dangerous.'

'I am not prepared to believe it.'

Zorlan's face was inscrutable. 'It might be a good thing to dispose of him before he can get into more mischief.'

Biggles' expression hardened a little. 'Isn't that going rather far in view of such evidence as we have?'

The Professor spoke succinctly. 'Captain Bigglesworth, if that man is what I am now almost sure he is, he would destroy you with no more compunction than if you were a gnat that had settled on the back of his hand.'

'If by that you mean he's a spy I'm prepared to believe it. You say you are *almost* sure. I say that is not enough to condemn him. Beyond that I have nothing to say. My orders were plain. You are in charge of the operation. My responsibility is limited to your safe transportation and the preservation of the aircraft for that purpose.'

Zorlan went on in his softly modulated voice: 'I see from your expression that you do not approve my methods. Let us have no misunderstandings. I hold no personal animosity against this man Alfondari, whatever he may be; but if, in fact, he is an an enemy agent, the situation resolves itself into a matter of survival either for him or for us. He is engaged in a dangerous project —'

'So, it seems, are we.'

'I shall not deny that. But we cannot both win the trick. I have met such people as Alfondari before, and I can assure you that in order to succeed in his purpose he will allow no scruple to stand in his way. I feel the same way about him, and by this time he is, or should be, aware of it.'

Biggles nodded. 'I take your point. So where does that get us?'

'After all, what is one life compared with the many who may die should the people this man represents succeed in their object?'

'We don't know yet who he represents.'

'We need not look far for the villains.'

'Let's get down to brass tacks. You're talking about the people who would like to seize Zarat?'

'Yes.'

'And you think the sheikh would fight to prevent that?'

'I'm sure of it.'

'How can you be sure?'

Zorlan spoke slowly. 'He told me so himself. Wouldn't you fight in an effort to preserve your freedom and independence?'

'I have already done so.'

'Very well. The people of Zarat would have no chance. If they fight they will be wiped out of existence. There is no need to say more.'

'We were about to have something to eat when you came back.'

'Then let us do that. Other matters can wait. There is no urgency, but Alfondari must be watched constantly.'

'That will be done. We shall have to feed him. He appears to have brought nothing with him.'

'That is significant. He doesn't expect to be here for very long.'

'I had already worked that out.'

'We can afford to give him food and drink. To allow the man to starve to death would be a long and tedious process. I'm afraid I have been guilty of carelessness.'

'In what way?'

'When this alleged Colonel – for I doubt if he has any military rank – first announced his intention of accompanying us, I should have demanded to see his written authority.'

Biggles smiled cynically. 'He'd come prepared for that. If he's what we believe him to be he'd have the necessary documents, genuine or forgeries, in his pocket. He wouldn't be such a fool as to try to join us without them.'

'Yes, you are probably right. As by this time he must realise he's under suspicion, he won't be surprised if I ask him to produce them. Meanwhile let us have something to eat.'

'Would you rather go in the cabin or stay outside? It will be very hot in the machine.'

'Then let us eat outside.'

At the mention of the aircraft Biggles turned to look at it, tucked in as far as it could be manoeuvred under the palms. Now that the sun was well past its zenith the slowly moving shadows of the fronds were painting the fuselage and most of the wings with transverse bars of black which cut the outlines into sections, as nature has provided the body of a zebra with protective camouflage. But the nacelle was still in the clear, the wind-screen glinting and the metal fittings glowing like white neon lights.

He turned to the others. 'We could be spotted from the air,' he said thoughtfully. 'It might be worth while completing the job the palms are doing for us. There are plenty of dead fronds about. Ginger, you might collect some and arrange them over the exposed parts. It won't take many minutes. It may not be necessary, but I shall feel more comfortable if we're out of sight from top-sides. Give him a hand, Bertie, while I deal with the grub department. Watch out for scorpions. This is the sort of place they like.'

Ginger and Bertie went to work, Alfondari watching with sombre eyes what was going on. He said nothing.

Presently they had a light meal, drinking with it bottles of cold soda-water from the refrigerator, perhaps the perfect drink in a hot climate. Some was given to Alfondari, still sitting motionless at the foot of his palm, head thrust forward on his hands, looking like a lizard waiting for a fly.

The day wore on in an oppressive silence and an atmosphere charged with unknown danger. Professor Zorlan stayed with the others near the air-craft, saying he could not fail to hear the approach of the men for whom he was waiting. He admitted he did not know whether there would be one man or several.

The sun, turning to the colour of blood and distorted by haze to twice its normal size, was fast sinking into the purple horizon as if exhausted by its own blazing fury, when Biggles suddenly raised his head in a listening attitude, eyes questing the eastern sky.

'I hear an aircraft,' he said. He looked at the Professor. 'Could this be the man we're waiting for?'

'No.'

'You are sure?'

'Quite sure. He has no plane.'

A moving speck, reduced to the size of a mosquito by distance, appeared, seeming to be crawling up the band of pale turquoise that fringed the distant mountains, throwing them into sharp relief. All eyes watched it.

'It's coming here,' said Ginger. 'At least, we're dead on its course.'

A minute or two passed, the rising noise of the power unit cutting the air into rolling waves of sound.

'Jet,' said Ginger.

'It's a MIG,' decided Bertie, shading his eyes.

'Keep still everybody,' ordered Biggles crisply. To Alfondari, who had started to get up, he repeated with an edge on his voice: 'I said keep still.'

Alfondari glared. He put a hand in a side pocket of his jacket. Biggles' automatic was out in a flash, covering him. 'If you move as much as one yard, or raise a hand, I'll shoot you,' he said, speaking distinctly but without passion. The threat may have been all the more convincing for that. At all events, Alfondari sank back on his haunches and remained motionless.

The Russian, or Russian produced, single-seat jet fighter came on, its wail changing note slightly as it lost height. Any doubt about its objective was soon dispelled, for on reaching the ruin-covered mound it went into a steep bank. It circled it three times, crossed it and recrossed it, losing height all the time, touching perhaps a hundred feet at its lowest point.

On the ground nobody moved. That applied to Alfondari, still covered by Biggles' pistol. Whether Biggles would have carried out his threat had the man attempted to show himself is a matter for surmise. From his expression it is likely he would have done so.

'He won't dare to put that thing down on an unknown

surface,' guessed Bertie, referring of course to the pilot of the high-performance fighter.

His guess proved correct, for a few moments later the machine headed away in the direction from which it had come.

Everyone breathed again.

'Did the pilot see us do you think?' Zorlan asked Biggles.

'No.'

'Can you be sure?'

'Fairly sure. Had he done so he would almost certainly have made a closer inspection of this particular spot. Anyhow, in his position that's what I would have done. Of course, he may have taken photographs.'

'The aircraft had some marks on it. Did you recognise them?'

'No. The machine is a Russian type, but it has been supplied to most of the Soviet satellites. I saw the markings, but all I can say about them is I've never seen them before. One seldom sees a MIG on our side of the Iron Curtain.'

'What do you make of it?'

'It's possible the machine may have been on a routine patrol flight to check up if there was anyone here, although who would do that and for what purpose you're in a better position to know than me.'

'You think the visit was more or less accidental?'

'It could have been, although we are then faced with the odd coincidence that it should occur on the very day of our arrival. If you want my frank opinion, as I prefer not to trust coincidence, I would say it's more likely that Alfondari managed to transmit our position to someone before we realised what he had in his suitcase.'

With the MIG once more a speck in the final glow of sunset, Zorlan rose to his feet.

'What are you going to do?' asked Biggles.

'Ask Alfondari one or two pointed questions.'

'Do you expect him to tell the truth?'

'I shall know if he's lying.'

'We already know he's a liar.'

'The time has come when we must know exactly how we stand with him.'

Biggles said no more. Zorlan moved towards Alfondari.

'Good thing we decked our aircraft up with a bit of extra camouflage,' remarked Bertie.

'It was an obvious precaution after we discovered Alfondari had been signalling. I had a feeling we might have visitors.'

What Zorlan said to Alfondari the others did not know, being just out of earshot. Alfondari took some papers from his pocket. Zorlan read them and handed them back. After a brief conversation he rejoined Biggles' party.

'As you predicted, his papers appear to be in order,' he said. 'But that means nothing. It was lucky you found him using the radio when you did. Had he concealed the instrument, and himself, in the ruins, no doubt he would have spoken to the pilot of that plane. As things are, if the pilot didn't see us, he may have decided we were not here.'

'The immediate question is this: it will be dark in a few minutes. Assuming you intend to stay here, what are we going to do with Alfondari during the hours of darkness?'

'Can he do any more harm?'

'He might. He could slip away and hide in the ruins, pending the arrival of some of his friends. He might even try sniping at us if we went to look for him. He might damage the aircraft with the object of grounding us here.'

'Then he will have to be watched. For my part I must stay here for some days if necessary. This operation has taken a long time to arrange and it would be a pity to ruin it by impatience.'

For a few seconds the sun appeared to remain poised on the distant peaks, flooding the world with streaming crimson and extending the shadows of the palms far out across the wilderness, where the fronds, intertwining, created fantastic patterns; then it sank into the earth and night, sullen and menacing, took possession of the land.

'It's not going to be easy to watch Alfondari in this darkness,' stated Biggles uncomfortably.

'You'll hear him if he moves. The moon will rise presently. That should make the task easier.'

'My chief concern is the aircraft,' returned Biggles. He touched Ginger on the knee. 'Go and sit in the doorway of the cabin. You won't be able to see much until the moon comes up, but you should hear Alfondari if he comes near. Bertie can relieve you later.'

'Right.' Ginger moved off.

Some time passed in a silence that was profound, a hush so intense that all life on earth might have died. Then, to Biggles' relief, the silver orb of the moon floated up like a great shining bubble rising from a sea of black water. Its light, falling on a million pebbles lying on the face of the desert, set them glistening like gems. Alfondari was revealed still squatting hunched like a toad with his head sunk into arms folded across his knees. Zorlan lay stretched out, apparently asleep, or trying to sleep. Ginger sat on the cabin step facing Alfondari. Bertie sat beside Biggles, eyes brooding on the scene.

Time, regardless of the affairs of men, moved on. The moon soared majestically across its allotted course through a sky now ablaze with stars, each constellation playing the part assigned to it in a mighty scheme of creation beyond the understanding of mortals.

Biggles sent Bertie to relieve Ginger. 'Wake me in two hours,' he ordered.

CHAPTER 5

THE ENEMY STRIKES

TOWARDS dawn, when the sand and stones of the wilderness had given up the heat they had absorbed during the day, the thin air turned bitterly cold, so cold that only those who have experienced the shock of a drop in temperature of perhaps ninety degrees between sunset and sunrise can believe possible. Biggles, on guard, his teeth chattering, turned up his collar and tucked his hands into his arm-pits. Ginger, lying nearby, tried to snuggle deeper into the sand in a futile search for warmth. For the rest, the scene had remained unchanged, but the sleepers were now moving uneasily as the penetrating cold bit into their bones.

Ginger opened his eyes. 'Give me strength,' he moaned. 'This is murder.' He raised himself on an elbow. 'Everything okay?'

'Yes.'

'Alfondari?'

'He hasn't moved.'

'That surprises me.'

'It surprises me. Apparently he still has reasons for staying with us.'

The stars were fast losing their brilliance, and at the rustle of dry palm fronds as the dawn-wind caressed

them Biggles got up stiffly and stretched his muscles.
'I'll brew some coffee,' he said, and walking to the aircraft disappeared inside. By the time he reappeared, to
announce that coffee was ready for anyone who wanted
it, another day was being born in a riot of colour that
made the sky look as if a madman had been at work with
a box of paints.

There was a general movement towards the aircraft.
Only Alfondari remained seated.

'If you want some breakfast come and get it,' called
Biggles. 'I'm not going to wait on you.'

Alfondari rose to his feet and came over. From the
door Biggles handed him a cup of coffee and a plate of
biscuits. Alfondari took them, having of course to use
both hands. As Biggles released them he put a hand in
Alfondari's pocket and took out a small automatic. 'I
don't think you'll need this,' he said quietly. 'Leave it
with me until we get home in case you're tempted to do
something stupid.' It was all done in two seconds of
time. Strangely, perhaps, Alfondari made no attempt to
prevent this, although with both hands occupied he
could only have resisted by dropping his breakfast.

But his dark eyes, as they met Biggles', were heavy
with reproach. 'You think I'm a spy,' he said softly.

'I have every reason to think so,' returned Biggles
coolly.

'What about Zorlan?'

'What about him?'

'Isn't he a spy?'

'Maybe we're all spies if it comes to that,' parried
Biggles.

'Have you taken *his* pistol?'

'Assuming he carries one, no.'

'Why not? What is the difference between us?'

'He and I happen to be on the same side.'

'I would not be too sure of that,' replied Alfondari, darkly.

'Meaning what?'

'He has only one side – his own.' With that Alfondari walked back to his tree, leaving Biggles to ponder, somewhat uneasily, the implied accusation.

'What was that about?' asked Zorlan, when Biggles joined him on a little hillock that commanded a view of the eastern desert.

'I took his pistol.'

'Why?'

'He could have done some mischief with it. One bullet in the aircraft, in a fuel tank for instance, could keep us grounded here.'

'Did he object?'

'Not seriously. I had taken it before he realised what was happening. Anyhow, I feel more comfortable with that gun in my own pocket. What are you going to do?'

'Wait. There's nothing else we can do.'

Biggles went back to Bertie and Ginger. 'On your feet,' he requested. 'We might as well be doing something. Now the shadows are falling the other way it might be a good thing to pile a bit more camouflage on the aircraft in case that MIG comes back for another look round.'

Bertie looked up. 'You really think it will?'

'I'd bet on it. We've been warned. I'd say from now on someone is going to keep this pile of dust and rocks under observation.'

For half an hour they busied themselves on the machine, making it difficult, if not impossible, to be seen from above. The work was stopped by a call from Zorlan.

'I think I see my friends coming,' he said, as Biggles made haste to join him. He pointed. Far out in the desert there was a little cloud of dust.

'How do you know they're the right people?' asked Biggles dubiously.

'If they were enemies they would be in greater force. Moreover, as you see, they are approaching openly.'

Biggles shrugged. 'If you're satisfied I shall have to be.'

Zorland picked up his portfolio, without which he never moved, and started off up the mound. 'I shall be waiting for them when they arrive. The business should not take long.'

Biggles beckoned to Bertie and Ginger. Watching, presently they were able to make out five horsemen riding at a sharp canter.

Said Biggles, without enthusiasm: 'Zorlan seems to think this is what we've been waiting for. I hope he's right, because if he is it means we should soon be away from here. The more I see of this dump the less I like it. Keep an eye on Alfondari.'

However, Alfondari made no attempt to move as the little cavalcade came on, slowing its pace as it drew near, and finally, at a walk, disappeared from sight beyond the curve of the mound. What happened after that was not known, but it was presumed that contact had been made with Zorlan and a conference of some sort was now taking place.

The best part of half an hour passed without any change in the situation and Biggles was beginning to show signs of impatience, for he still feared the return of the MIG which he could only regard as hostile, when there occurred an interruption from an unexpected quarter. He stopped in his stride facing east when faintly through the thin air came the drone of an aircraft. The others got up and stared in the same direction.

After a long pause he said: 'Can you see him?'

'I can't,' answered Bertie.

'Nor me,' murmured Ginger. 'But I can tell you this, he added. 'That isn't a MIG. It's a piston-engined job.'

Biggles' eyes were now searching other points of the compass. They stopped facing north-west. 'There he is,' he said. 'He's coming towards us dead on so it can only mean he's coming here. Now what? I'd bet my boots this means trouble.'

'Why should it?' queried Ginger. 'We're in order in being here.'

'For what possible reason would a machine come to this out-of-the-way dump unless it had business with us? We're nowhere near a regular route. If someone's coming to see us it won't be to bring good news.'

It could now be seen that the fast-approaching machine was a twin-engined high-wing monoplane.

'Anyone know the type?' asked Biggles. 'I don't remember seeing those square-cut wing tips before.'

Neither Ginger nor Bertie could supply the information.

All they could do was stand still while the plane came on, losing height, with the hill obviously its objective. After a quick reconnaissance it landed and ran to a stop as close as it could conveniently get, a matter of twenty to thirty yards. Guns projecting from the leading edge of the wings showed it to be a military type.

Biggles took a deep breath of relief when it came

broadside on to reveal the identification marks of the Turkish Air Force: a plain red square on the fuselage with a white crescent and star against a red background on the fin. 'I wonder what brings *him* here,' he murmured in a puzzled voice. 'Actually, unless he has a visa for Zarat he has no right to land here.'

'He may be having engine trouble, or perhaps lost his way,' suggested Ginger.

'I doubt it. He didn't act like that.'

The explanation was soon forthcoming. Two men, officers judging from their uniforms, got out, leaving the motors ticking over. One stayed by the machine; the other advanced. There was nothing aggressive in his manner.

Reaching the spectators he saluted smartly. 'Captain Bigglesworth?' he queried.

Biggles took a pace forward. 'Can I help you?'

'I am from the Turkish Intelligence Service at Ankara,' was the answer, in fair English but with a marked accent. 'I believe you have in your expedition a certain Colonel Alfondari. You picked him up on the airport at Ankara.'

Biggles smiled. 'It would be more correct to say he picked us up. He informed us that he had been detailed by the Turkish authorities to act as our escort. Naturally, being in no position to dispute this, we accepted him.'

The officer smiled cynically. 'Did it not occur to you that he might be a spy?'

'At the time, no. Why should anyone want to spy on us?'

The officer shrugged. 'No matter. We have come to take him away. We had been watching him, but he escaped us. We made inquiries and learned that he had been seen to get in your plane just before it took off. Where is he?'

Biggles pointed to where Alfondari, who through all this had not moved, sat under his tree. 'There he is. I'm sorry if in some way —'

The officer brushed the apology aside. 'You are not to blame. We will take him away and see that he does not trouble you again. Good morning.' Another salute and the speaker strode purposefully towards Alfondari. Reaching him he spoke sharply. Alfondari got up, and after a short conversation the two of them walked to the aircraft. They got in. The pilot climbed back into his cockpit. The engines were revved up. The machine turned, raising a great cloud of dust; then it was away, heading in the direction from which it had come.

'What about that, eh?' chuckled Bertie. 'So we're rid of Alfondari. Jolly good. These jolly old Turks are smart on the job, what?'

Biggles was watching the aircraft. He did not answer. He was not smiling.

Bertie looked at him curiously. 'Something wrong, old boy?'

'I don't know,' replied Biggles, slowly and pensively. 'But the thought has just struck me that we may have been taken for a jaunt up the garden path.'

'I don't get it.'

'Things may not be quite what they seem.'

'Such as?'

'How do we know that aircraft was Turkish, or that fellow was what he pretended to be – a Turkish officer?'

'With those markings the machine couldn't be anything else but Turkish.'

'Couldn't it? Anyone can slap some paint on any aircraft.'

'What are you getting at?'

'I may be getting a bit slow on the uptake, but now I've had time to think a feeling grows on me that neither that machine nor its crew were what they appeared to be. I have a suspicion they were pals of Alfondari, sent here to pick him up.'

'For crying out loud!' exclaimed Ginger. 'What put that idea in your head?'

'Several things, none of them significant in itself but taken together add up to something I can't ignore. To start with, Alfondari showed no surprise, and certainly no alarm, when that aircraft landed. Why? He must have seen the Turkish markings. If he was a fraud, pretending to be Turkish, surely that would have worried him. Why didn't it? Was it because he expected someone to come and take him home – wherever that might be? He knew we suspected him of being a spy, yet he sat here as quiet as a lamb. He knew there was no need for him to do anything. He went off without the slightest protest. If I'm right he must now be laughing at the way we were taken in. There was nothing we could have done about it even if we had suspected this earlier. We couldn't have prevented the machine from leaving. As you must have noticed, the pilot never left it.'

'We could have prevented it from taking Alfondari,' said Bertie.

'By resorting to force, perhaps, which would probably have meant a shooting match. What would have been the sense of that? We don't want Alfondari. I'm glad to be rid of him. He'd become a responsibility. Don't overlook the fact that the aircraft carried guns.

The men with it must have seen our machine when they were on the ground. We should have looked silly had they taken off and shot it to pieces from the air. Taking it all by and large I think we're better off as things are.'

Ginger spoke. 'There was no need for Alfondari to stay with us any longer. He knows what's going on here, or as much as he's ever likely to know. He did what he came to do and it looks as if he's got away with it. It's my guess that the people behind him knew something had gone wrong with their plan. Look at it like this. They must have known Alfondari had a radio transmitter. That being so they'd be sitting on the right wave-length waiting for his signals. They started to come through. Then, suddenly, they cut out. Moreover, they were not resumed. Why? The answer's pretty obvious. We had spotted what Alfondari was up to and put a stop to it. That, in fact, is exactly what did happen. It follows that once we'd realised our passenger was a spy, there would be no point in leaving him here. No more signals could be expected, but if he could be brought home he'd be able to talk. So a plane was sent to pick him up. Once it gets to its base Alfondari will be able to do all the talking he would no doubt have done from here had we not silenced his radio. I'd say it's as simple as that.'

Biggles nodded gloomily, his eyes still on the aircraft under discussion, now a fast-fading speck in the sky. 'That's about the English of it. The course that plane is on won't take it to Ankara, or anywhere near it. We may be wrong, but if we're right we should soon know all about it. The devil of it is, Alfondari knows the people Zorlan came here to meet are here at this very moment. We can reckon the machine he's in is equipped with radio. You realise what that means. He has only to send a signal to his headquarters and this hump of dirt we're sitting on will be about as healthy as a dynamite factory that's just caught fire. It looks as if the ruins of Quarda are due for a bit more knocking about.'

'Then it's time we were on our way,' said Bertie brightly.

'We can't go without Zorlan. What the deuce is he doing? He behaves as if time didn't matter.'

'If he knew what had happened here he might be persuaded to step out a bit faster,' suggested Ginger.

'Probably. Our orders were to stay here, but in the circumstances I think he should be told what has happened. It could affect the entire transaction – whatever that might be. Ginger, hoof it to the top of the hill and see if you can spot him. If you can find him tell him what goes on.'

'Right.' Ginger set off up the hill at a run, dodging the obstacles.

The others watched him. Once or twice he disappeared from sight behind masses of old masonry, but for a moment near the top he stood in plain view. There he stopped, staring towards the east. Then he looked down at them, arm outstretched, pointing in the same direction. He followed this by making a signal that was not understood except that it indicated urgency. His voice reached them faintly, but what he called was heard neither by Biggles nor Bertie, for at that moment a slight breeze was stirring the palm fronds causing them to rustle harshly; and, of course, the nearer sounds drowned the more distant one.

'What do you make of that?' muttered Biggles, as Ginger appeared to dive over a ridge.

'I'd say he's spotted Zorlan. What else could it mean? It's a bit soon to expect trouble.'

'If that jet we saw is based not far behind those hills on the horizon it could be here within ten minutes of getting a signal from Alfondari,' returned Biggles with an anxiety he did not attempt to conceal.

At that moment the breeze died away and Ginger's behaviour was explained. It came with the wail of jets, as yet far off but rising swiftly to the crescendo produced when aircraft so equipped are diving.

Biggles looked up but could see nothing, which told him that the machines were already low; so he dashed to a point that commanded a view of the direction from which the howl was coming. One glance was enough. He ran back. 'MIGs – three of 'em. Take cover,' he snapped and threw himself flat as close as he could get to the bottom of a block of stone.

Bertie lay beside him.

They were just in time. Within seconds it seemed that all hell had been let loose. Guns were crackling like castanets and bullets ripping through palms, ploughing up the sand or flying off the old stones in screaming ricochets. The noise of this, combined with the scream of jets as they swooped low, was shattering. Biggles twisted his body so that he could see the Merlin and watched for it to become a definite target. He heard a few bullets hit it, but where he did not know. He thought they were stray shots, inevitable as the entire hill seemed to be under fire. He got the impression that the shooting, in the absence of an conspicuous objective, was at random. The aircraft, well camouflaged as it was, would not be easy to pick out by jets flying almost at ground

level at top speed. Occasionally he caught a momentary
glimpse of one as it flashed past.

He did not speak. Neither did Bertie. For one thing
there was nothing to be said, and for another the noise
was such that conversation would have been impossible.

Once Bertie touched Biggles on the arm and pointed.
Five loose horses were tearing madly across the wilderness. One fell. It tried to get up but fell again and lay
still. It may have been struck by a bullet or it may have
tripped over its broken reins and broken its neck. The
other four raced on, scattering.

The attack lasted about five minutes. Then the MIGs
withdrew. Hearing them going, Biggles took a cautious
peep. 'All over,' he told Bertie. 'They're away.'

Bertie got into a sitting position and wiped his
monocle. 'I say, old boy, that was pretty hot. The bligh-
ters did their best to make a right job of it.'

'They didn't waste any time getting here,' growled
Biggles. 'I was expecting trouble but nothing quite on
that scale. Ginger must have seen 'em coming. I hope he
had the sense to find himself a good hole to lie up in.
Let's have a look at the aircraft. That was my big worry.
I don't think they saw it.'

Having satisfied themselves that the attackers were
clear away, they walked over to it and made a quick
inspection. They found two holes in a wing, three in the
tail unit and one had gone right through the cabin. But
as far as they could make out no serious damage had
been done. There was no sign of leaking oil or petrol.

'Here comes Ginger, so he's all right,' observed
Bertie.

Biggles lit a cigarette. 'Good. Let's hear what he has to
say about it.'

CHAPTER 6

QUESTIONS WITHOUT ANSWERS

GINGER came bouncing down the slope in long strides, his face wearing a grin that looked forced.

'Everything okay?' he questioned anxiously as he joined the others.

'More or less,' replied Biggles. 'You seem to be all right. I was worried about you.'

'When I saw what was coming, no rabbit with a dog on its tail went to ground faster than I did. I took a header between some rocks and stayed here. Gosh! What a carry-on!'

'What about Zorlan and the rest?'

'I don't know.'

'Why not?'

'I haven't seen them.'

'Didn't you see them before the shooting started?'

'No. I had a look round from the top of the hump but they weren't in sight. Naturally, when those MIGs started plastering the place I didn't do any more looking. I saw the horses. They'd been left tethered to a palm at the bottom of the slope on the far side.'

'They stampeded.'

'No wonder.'

'They'll take some catching. The last we saw of them they were making flat out for the horizon, each one going its own way.'

'That's dandy. What will Zorlan and Co. do about that?'

'Here he comes now,' put in Bertie. 'Maybe he'll tell us.'

Professor Zorlan, still carrying his portfolio, came striding down the hill. For once he was hurrying. His expression, when he came up, was more austere than usual. 'No doubt we can thank Alfondari for that exhibition,' he said in a voice venomous with anger. He looked round. 'Where is he?'

'He's gone,' informed Biggles calmly.

'Gone! Gone where? How could he go?'

'A Turkish military aircraft, or a plane showing Turkish nationality marks, landed here and picked him up. You must have heard it.'

'I heard something, but I naturally assumed it was you testing your engines.'

'I had no reason to test them. The officer in charge introduced himself as from Turkish Intelligence Headquarters at Ankara. Alfondari had been seen getting into our plane. The man, he said, was a spy, and he had come to collect him.'

'So he took him away?'

'He did.'

'You didn't try to prevent it?'

'I did not. Why should I? I was glad to see the back of Alfondari. He'd become a nuisance.'

'I take it you believed what this officer told you?'

'At first I had no reason to doubt it. Taken by surprise, we were in a difficult position. The last thing I thought you'd want was trouble with the Turkish authorities. Had the plane been what it claimed to be, and I had refused to let Alfondari go, it could have started something. In any case I could see no point in saddling ourselves any longer with a man we couldn't trust. I thought we were well rid of him.'

'You talk as if you have doubts about this plane?'

'I have now.' Biggles gave his reasons.

Zorlan bit his lip. 'We should have shot the man at once when we realised he was a spy.'

'Say we suspected it. We weren't sure. You can't shoot a man on suspicion.'

'I take no chances.'

'I can see that. What good would it have done?' returned Biggles coldly. 'It wouldn't have stopped that plane coming here. What could I have told the officer in charge to account for Alfondari's disappearance? It was known he was with us. Had I said we'd killed him, and it then turned out he was a Turkish national, it's likely we should have seen the inside of a Turkish gaol. But instead of standing here wasting time talking about what we *might* have done, wouldn't it be better to decide what we're going to do? What of the party you met on the hill? Presumably you had no casualties.'

'We were never in danger. To take advantage of the shade we were negotiating our business in one of the excavated houses.'

'I hope you got what you came for.'

'Up to a point, yes.'

'You know the horses have gone?'

'Yes.'

'We saw them go. You'll have a job to find them. One

I think was killed. The others must be miles away by now. How are your friends going to get back to where they came from?'

'I have already discussed that with them. They can't be expected to walk nearly thirty miles across the open desert, in this heat, to the nearest fresh water, so you will have to fly them.'

Biggles' face fell. 'I can't say I'm infatuated with that idea. You realise that if those MIGs come back and catch us in the open we've had it. We couldn't even put up a fight.'

'There's no alternative. It's a risk that must be taken.'

Biggles took a cigarette from a pack and tapped it on his thumb nail. 'Don't you think, Professor Zorlan, that it's time we were told what this is all about? Surely the time for secrecy has passed. It isn't that I'm inquisitive or even curious. I'm not concerned with Middle Eastern potentates or politics, but I feel that as we're on the job we might as well do the best we can with it. It's more to your advantage than ours, I think, that we should succeed; but this waffling about in unknown country without knowing where we're going next, or why, isn't making things any easier for me. I know I'm here to take your instructions, and I'm prepared to do that; but the more I know what all this is in aid of, as we used to say in the R.A.F., the better shall I be able to cope with an emergency should it arise. At present I'm by no means sure who are our friends and who our enemies. Who are those people on the hill? It's pretty obvious that somebody knows; but we don't.' Having thus disclosed what was in his mind, Biggles lit the cigarette.

After a pause for reflection Zorlan answered. 'Your

argument may be justified. Very well. One of the men on the hill is the Sheikh of Zarat. With him is his Prime Minister and Foreign Secretary. The other two are attendants – bodyguards if you like.'

'Thank you. So now we know. Now may I make a suggestion?'

'I shall be interested to hear it.'

'The sooner we're away from here the better. Those MIGs may repeat their attack, or it's even possible a ground force may be sent here. In fact I'm pretty sure of it.'

'Why are you sure?'

'It's known we have an aircraft here. Some people, including Alfondari, knew about the machine before it left Ankara. Alfondari knows where it is now. That means other people know. Hence the attack. One purpose of that may have been to destroy our aircraft and so keep us here, or at least curtail our movements. It must be known by now that the aircraft was not destroyed. Had it been, those MIG pilots would have seen the smoke. In case you've never seen a burning aircraft, I can tell you it puts up a considerable cloud of black smoke.'

'Very well. Let say those planes came over to destroy our aircraft and failed.'

'Did you see them?'

'Not clearly. Did you?'

'Clearly enough.'

'So you know where they came from?'

'Not definitely. All I know is they carried the Red Star, which means they came from one of the Communist countries. Which one I couldn't say. Russia has supplied MIGs to most of her satellites. Never mind. It isn't really important. It comes to the same thing in the end. What I would like to know is why all this fuss suddenly to put out of action a civil plane that's minding its own business? Or was there another reason, a more serious one, in coming here?'

'It is possible.'

'So you know what it is.'

'Yes.'

'Is someone trying to kill the sheikh and his ministers?'

'It might well be.'

'Why? What has the sheikh done?'

'He has done nothing.'

'That doesn't make sense to me. People don't go out of their way to commit murder for no reason at all. Could it be that someone has put up a proposition to him and he has turned it down?'

'If you must know that is precisely what has happened.'

'The proposition could only be concerned with Zarat. Which means there must be something here more valuable than what I see on the surface.'

'How persistent you are. Does it matter?'

'Only to the extent that, as I said just now, I'd be in a better position to set my clock right if I knew what these people were after.'

'Can't you guess? What is the wealth that is pouring out of the ground in so many Middle Eastern countries?'

Understanding dawned in Biggles' eyes. 'Oil! Great Scott! So that's it. Where oil flows so does blood, mostly the blood of innocent people to whom the accursed stuff means nothing except hard labour in the refineries.'

Zorlan shrugged. 'Now you know. I trust you are satisfied. Anything else?'

'That's all I need to know. Now let's see about getting out of this.'

'It would be advisable.'

'Where are we going?'

'That has already been decided. My first business with the sheikh is finished and it only remains to get him home safely and as quickly as possible. That does not mean we need take him all the way to the palace at Zarana, the capital. That could be dangerous, for there might be spies watching even there. About twenty-five miles due east from where we stand there is an oasis called Suwara. It is occupied by a small outpost of the sheikh's troops. The sheikh uses it as a centre for hunting. He says all will be well if we take him there. The oasis is surrounded by *sabkha*, so there will be no difficulty in landing. Men will be sent out to recapture the lost horses, although being desert-bred they will probably make their way home.'

'That's quite clear,' stated Biggles. 'Having landed our passengers, what then? Do we go home?'

'I'm afraid not.'

Biggles looked startled. 'Don't say we're to come back here!'

'That depends on circumstances. Not immediately, anyway. Our next move will be to fly to Rasal al Sharab.'

Biggles frowned, searching his memory, and recalled this was the possible second objective mentioned by the Air Commodore. 'That's the other little independent state lying farther south, near the frontiers of Iraq and Iran?' he queried.

'Correct.'

'And what do we do there?'

'Pick up a passenger.'

'For where?'

'For here – that is, Zarat.'

Biggles smiled bleakly. 'A shuttle service over this sort of territory, without an airfield, isn't my idea of a jolly life, but if that's what you want it's all right with me. Shall we get on with it? When we get to the oasis does it matter where we land?'

'No, so long as it's as close as possible. The oasis isn't a large one. I'll fetch the sheikh. I advised him to stay where he was for the moment, until you were quite ready, in case those aircraft paid us a return visit. While I'm away you'd better take the opportunity of having a quick lunch.'

'What about you? Don't you need food?'

'No. I'm accustomed to going for long periods without any.'

'And the sheikh?'

'No doubt he will eat something when he gets to the oasis.'

'As you say. We'll clear this rubbish off the plane.'

Zorlan set off up the mound.

'He certainly is a queer bird,' observed Bertie.

'Let's grab some grub while we can,' advised Biggles. 'The way things are going we may end up without any.'

Some twenty minutes later they were clearing the camouflage off the aircraft when Ginger remarked: 'Here they come.'

They all made a searching inspection of the party that now came down the hill with Zorlan leading.

'What do you make of 'em?' asked Bertie.

Biggles shrugged. 'Don't ask me. I think their skins are too light for them to be Arabs. They look more like Caucasians. It doesn't matter to us what they are.'

The party arrived at the aircraft. There were no introductions, but from his authoritative bearing there was no doubt as to which was the sheikh. He bowed courteously to the airmen. He was a good-looking young man of slight build with blue eyes that seemed strangely out of place with a semi-oriental style of dress, noticeably a short red jacket, baggy trousers fastened in at the ankle, and a yellow turban. He wore a small black beard and a moustache. The jewelled sheath of a dagger was suspended from his waist by a gold chain. The bodyguards were tall, fierce-looking men with upturned moustaches, like buffalo horns. Each carried a rifle. Bandoliers filled with cartridges crossed their chests. Scimitars, the single-edged curved swords peculiar to the Middle East, hung at their sides.

'Real musical comedy stuff,' breathed Ginger in Biggles' ear.

'I wouldn't care to count on that,' returned Biggles soberly.

'Are you ready?' inquired Zorlan curtly.

'I have only to start the engines.'

'Then let us go.'

Leaving Ginger to make the party comfortable in the cabin, in which of course he himself would have to travel, Biggles climbed into the cockpit, where Bertie joined him saying: 'Are we going to have any difficulty finding this oasis?'

'I wouldn't think so. Zorlan said it was twenty-five miles due east, and there can't be so many oases that we're likely to make a mistake.' Biggles started the engines. 'While you're making sure they're ready inside, you might have a last look round to make certain there are no MIG's about.'

Bertie did so. 'All clear,' he reported.

'Then we'll press on.' Biggles advanced the throttle and the aircraft, tail up and swiftly gathering speed, raced across the open plain. Having such a short distance to go, he did not climb to any altitude. At a thousand feet he levelled out, all the time keeping a close watch on the sky, and in three minutes an oasis was in sight. There was only one, so it could not be other than Suwara, the objective. A narrow belt of bright green palms, presumably round a water-hole, it made a refreshing spot of colour in the drab wilderness, very different from the sun-parched ruins they had just left.

'If there's one thing in the world that looks exactly as you imagined it, it's an oasis,' remarked Bertie, scanning the sky.

'And they're all alike,' contributed Biggles, as he cut the engines and having glided in touched down on the near side, allowing the plane to run to a standstill near the palms. Some men ran out to look at them but did not advance.

Leaving the engines ticking over he got down. 'Is this the place?' he asked Zorlan, who was first out of the cabin.

'Yes.'

'Are we to stay here?'

'Yes.'

'For how long?'

'I don't know. Long enough for the sheikh to see if

there is any news from the palace. He thinks it might be better for you to wait here until sundown before flying on.'

'For what reason?'

'There would be less risk of you being seen.'

'That won't make much difference. We shall be heard, anyhow.'

'I'll speak to him about it.'

'According to my information Rasal al Sharab is two hundred miles from here.'

'About that.'

'Then you might point out that if we don't leave here until sundown it will mean landing in the dark.'

'Does that worry you?'

'I'd rather land on unknown ground in daylight.'

'Very well. Those enemy planes have upset the arrangements. Had they not interfered it would not have been necessary to come here.'

'Are you coming with us?'

'Certainly. The two bodyguards also.'

'Why them?'

'They will escort the passenger we are to pick up and bring back here.'

'Do you mean here or the ruins of Quarda?'

'That has yet to be decided. It will depend on news, if any, the sheikh learns here.'

'Is he staying here?'

'Unless he finds it necessary to go to his palace. Horses are available. In that case he will return as soon as possible. If for any reason it would be dangerous for us to land here on our return from Rasal al Sharab we shall be warned by rockets.'

'And in that case?'

'We shall have to go on to Quarda.' Zorlan strode away, following the sheikh and his staff who by this time had walked into the oasis and disappeared between the date palms.

Bertie looked at Biggles helplessly. What a to-do! What do you make of it?'

'You know as much as I do.'

'This oil business was a bit of an eye-opener. We weren't told anything about that.'

'It wasn't necessary. I realised the basic idea of all this juggling was a mutual assistance plan between Zarat and Rasal al Sharab. Now we see the reason for it. Until now neither country had anything worth grabbing, but if someone has struck oil it becomes a very different proposition. No wonder the tigers are sneaking up smacking their lips.'

Said Ginger: 'I can tell you one thing.'

'And what's that?'

'The sheikh speaks English as well as we do – probably better. He has an accent commonly known as Oxford.'

'How do you know?'

'On the way here he started to talk in English to Zorlan; but he didn't get a chance to say much. Zorlan butted in and stopped him, presumably because I was there. After that they spoke in another language. That may mean nothing, but I couldn't help wondering what it was Zorlan didn't want me to hear.'

'This particular sheikh wouldn't be the first one to go to an English university. I couldn't care less about that. What worries me is we seem to have become responsible for him, and as that's the sort of responsibility I don't like I shall be glad to see the end of it all and get back home.

Too many people know what's going on here, with the result that the place must be fairly crawling with enemy agents under orders to scotch our game – if you can call it a game – at any cost. Anyhow, as we're in it up to the neck we shall have to see it through. Zorlan has opened up a little, but I'm pretty sure he still hasn't told us the whole story. I imagine the rest is in that portfolio he carries. He takes good care to see no one gets a chance to open it.'

'What could be in it?' conjectured Ginger.

'Papers, obviously. Perhaps a proposal for some sort of agreement with Zarat or Rasal al Sharab. Possibly a concession to work the oil in return for financial aid. But what's the use of guessing? It doesn't matter to us what's in the bag. We're only here to cart it around. Let's have a drink while we're waiting.'

CHAPTER 7

NATURE TAKES A HAND

IT was nearly two hours before Zorlan returned. With him came the two bodyguards, their faces expressionless. They may have looked like characters in a musical comedy, as Ginger had remarked, but he decided to take no chances of falling out with them. He suspected the scimitars had an edge and were not being worn as ornaments.

'You've been a long time,' Biggles greeted Zorlan.

'It seems there has been a little trouble at the palace, but everything is now under control.'

'What was the trouble?'

'A plot to assassinate the sheikh. It was forestalled.'

'Did you speak to the sheikh about our time of departure?'

'Yes. He is satisfied to leave the decision to you.'

'Good. Tell me this. Are we expected at Rasal al Sharab?'

'Yes. That is, when the plane is seen its purpose will be known and final preparations made. A plane rarely calls there.'

'What about these guards? Are they really necessary?'

'They might be.'

'That's a comforting thought,' said Biggles with mild sarcasm. 'Can you speak their language?'

'Yes.'

'That's something anyway.'

'They will identify Rasal al Sharab if there is any doubt. Were you given instructions for finding the place?'

'I was given a map and a compass course in relation to Quarda by my chief in case it should be needed.'

'There should be no difficulty. Rasal is a town of some size, as towns in this part of the world go. The sultan's palace is really a fort. Standing in open ground it should be conspicuous.'

'How long are we likely to be there?'

'I can't tell you. I have some business to do with the sultan before we collect our passenger; but you can rely on me to get away as quickly as possible.'

'Which means you'll be leaving us?'

'For a time, yes.'

'What about the guards?'

'They will come with me to protect the passenger.'

'Fair enough.'

'Any more questions?'

'No. That's all. If you're ready we might as well get along. We're just as likely to be seen here standing in the open, should an enemy aircraft come over, as in the desert.'

Biggles saw his passengers into their seats, climbed into his own and started the engines. They needed no warming. The time, he noticed, was four o'clock, which meant that the sun would be low by the time they reached the objective.

'We should be there in half an hour or so,' he told

Bertie, as he unfolded his map to refresh his memory.
Having done so he refolded it in its creases and put it
handy in the pocket beside him. 'Have a look round,' he
requested as he taxied into position for the take-off.

'Can't see anything,' reported Bertie. 'I imagine any
MIGs about will be operating between their base and
Quarda.'

'I wouldn't care to gamble too much on that. If one of
'em lands at the ruins and discovers their raid was a flop
they'll want to know where we've gone. As that would
mean a general reconnaissance over the whole region we
might run into one anywhere. Remember that to get to
Rasal we shall have to cut across a bit of the north-east
corner of Iraq. I don't know how we stand with the
Iraqis, but they may have a finger in this unsavoury pie
and might have been alerted. I'd feel a lot happier if we
had some guns to hit back at anyone who had a smack at
us, but I suppose the Turkish government wouldn't risk
trouble by allowing a foreign military machine to fly
over their territory.'

'The MIGs are doing it.'

'That's different. The Iron Curtain lot are powerful
enough to cock a snook at anyone and get away with it.
Smaller countries have to think twice before falling out
with 'em and you can't blame them for that. Well, let's
see what the luck's like.' So saying he took off, and
swinging round put the aircraft on its course.

Again he held the machine low, knowing he would be
less likely to be seen from above against the uneven
background than if he were high in the sky. He would of
course be more easily seen from the ground, but he was
fairly confident he would be unlikely to encounter opposition from that direction, even if there was anyone

there. Natives, in camp or on a journey, perhaps, but they hardly counted. Hostile aircraft were the real danger; and being an old hand at air combat he did not need telling that by flying low the shadow of the machine, racing along beside him, being black and therefore more conspicuous than the aircraft itself, would be smaller than if cast from a higher altitude. The only objection was, in the hot, thin, unstable air, the machine bumped at every irregularity in the ground. He did his best to control this, but it could not be entirely prevented. He could only hope his passengers would not be sick.

For the first part of the trip the terrain was much as it had been in the vicinity of Quarda and the oasis of Suwara; that is to say, a vast desolation of sterile, gravelly soil, so arid that it could support no vegetation except sparse growths of the inevitable camel-thorn; but at about half-way it began to change its character. The desert aspect persisted, but it became increasingly broken by gullies torn in the earth by storm-water where there was nothing in the ground to hold the soil together. For the most part these signs of erosion ran more or less parallel with the line of flight showing which way the land fell, and eventually, as Biggles expected, having seen this sort of country before, they became dry tributaries, so to speak, of a wide, shallow *wadi* – the same thing on a larger scale.

The chief difference was the *wadi* held a certain amount of vegetation in the form of another hardy inhabitant of desert places, acacia thorn. It grew as isolated bushes or in widely scattered clumps and probably indicated the existence of water, although it might have been deep in the ground.

As the aircraft raced on these became more common, and Biggles formed the opinion that as the *wadi* fell in the direction he was travelling it would probably take him to Rasal al Ahrab. If there was water, even under the ground provided it could be reached by wells, it would account for the existence of a town in the middle of a wilderness.

All this of course made no difference to the aircraft as long as there was sufficient open ground on which he would be able to land when he reached his destination. The uneven ground merely caused the machine to rock a little more erratically as an up-current struck the underside of one of the wings. When the entire machine was affected it reacted by bouncing, sickening for those unaccustomed to the movement.

It may be that with the dominant risk of interference coming from the air Biggles had given no thought to the natural hazards of flying from which no country is entirely free. Taking the functional perfection of the aircraft for granted, there are always local weather conditions which man has not yet mastered and probably never will. In temperate zones, as everyone knows, the worst hazards are fog and ice-forming conditions. In hot countries, particularly those subject to monsoons, it can be tempests of such violence that rain or hail can reduce visibility to zero. In the great deserts of the world the peril is wind-borne sand which can be carried to a great height. This, too, may completely blot out whatever may be underneath. And that is not the only danger.

The Merlin had completed about two-thirds of its journey and Biggles was studying the ground and sky in turn when Bertie called his attention to something that was happening ahead. A dark shadow, almost black in the centre, appeared to be hanging over a section of the horizon. Biggles took a long look at it and then glanced at the sun. It had lost its glare and showed as a pale orange globe.

He swore softly. 'Looks as if we're running into a *haboob*,'* he muttered. 'What a curse. We just needed that.'

'What are we going to do about it?'

'There's no point in doing anything until we see which way it's going.'

'It looks to me as if it's dead on our course, coming towards us. Could we get round it?'

'Possibly, by going miles out of our way.'

'How about getting above it?'

'That could mean going up to twelve or fifteen thousand.'

'Does that matter?'

'We wouldn't be able to get down at Rasal while the storm is on and it may last for hours. Then we should have to wait for the dust to settle. Instead of burning petrol we can't afford, it might be better to sit down here in the *wadi* and wait for it to pass. That's if we can find a slice of open ground long enough.' Biggles looked down at the ground to survey the floor of the *wadi* in front of them.

In an instant the aircraft was standing on a wing tip in a vertical bank.

'What the devil . . .!' exclaimed Bertie, grabbing at his seat to steady himself.

* *Haboob*. Native name for a fast-moving sand-storm, often of devastating violence, common in the deserts of North Africa and the Middle East.

'There are two shadows on the ground – we're only making one,' answered Biggles tersely. 'Can you spot him?'

Somewhere, faintly, a machine gun snarled. A line of tracer bullets, well clear of the Merlin, ploughed into the bed of the *wadi*.

Bertie's eyes back-tracked the line. 'MIG,' he shouted. 'Coming down starboard quarter!'

Biggles dived for the ground, twisting like a wounded bird. Straightening below the banks of the *wadi* he flicked on full throttle and tore along the bottom. In less than a minute he was in a brown murk which increased in density every second. He lowered his wheels shouting: 'Where is he?'

'Can't see him. Unless he's nuts he'll never follow us into this stuff. If he does he'll be into the carpet before he sees it.'

'If I can find a place I'm going down.'

'Why not up and get over it?'

'Not with that MIG about. If he caught us in the clear it'd be curtains for us. Go aft and tell Zorlan we're running into a *haboob* with a MIG on our tail.'

'Ha! That should cheer him.' Bertie disappeared through the door into the cabin.

Biggles, peering into the gloom, moistened his lips. The sun had vanished. Brown clouds were swirling past bringing a dim twilight, but he could still see the floor of the *wadi* due to the wind carrying the sand over it without giving it a chance to settle. Even so, visibility was less than a hundred yards and fast shortening. Ahead was a stretch of ground without, as far as he could see, bushes or other obstructions. What lay beyond he did not know, but realising it was now or never he cut the engines. He had one thing in his favour. The gale of wind was rushing straight up the *wadi*; it would pull him up quickly.

Bertie came back, flopped into his seat and fastened his safety belt. Seeing what was happening he did not speak.

With the aircraft sinking Biggles held his breath as he stared fixedly ahead. The wheels touched down. The machine bounced a little, then the wheels trundled. A dark object loomed in front. With its wheels ploughing into loose sand the machine came to a stop within yards of it. A clump of acacia scrub.

'In a flash Biggles had switched off and unfastened his belt. 'Get some rag and help me plug the air intakes,' he rapped out. 'A couple of spare shirts – anything. Buck up.'

Bertie dived into the cabin. In a matter of seconds he had joined Biggles on the ground with what was required. Holding handkerchiefs over their mouths and nostrils, flinching as the flying sand stung their eyes, they did what was necessary, after which they lost no time in getting back into their seats.

'What an absolute stinker,' growled Bertie, as he slammed the door to keep out as much sand as possible although some inevitably would find its way in. 'We're down, any old how, and that's something to be thankful for.'

'And if this blasted sand piles up on us we're likely to stay down,' returned Biggles grimly. 'What did Zorlan say when you told him how things stood?'

'Nothing much. He seemed a bit peeved at being thrown out of his seat when you did that cart-wheel turn.'

'He's damn lucky to be alive,' stated Biggles bitingly.

'I hope he realises it.'

'He will, because I shall tell him so if he starts moaning to me. Stay where you are while I have a word with him.'

'Will the machine be all right do you think?'

'Facing dead into wind it should be. We've no tackle to anchor it, anyhow. I'll be back.' Biggles went through into the cabin.

'Was this really necessary?' Zorlan greeted him caustically.

'Had I not thought so I wouldn't have done it,' answered Biggles shortly. 'There's nothing I can do about a *haboob* except get out of its way if that's possible. In this case it wasn't.'

'Why not?'

'For the very good reason that we were being dogged by an aircraft armed with machine guns. It had in fact already fired at us. My machine is not equipped for combat. You've nothing to complain about. We are at least on the ground in one piece. Kindly remember that I have a life to lose as well as you.'

'Where did the MIG go?'

'How could I know? Home if the pilot's got any sense. He'd be as helpless in this stuff as we are. Sand in an engine doesn't improve its performance.'

'The pilot will have guessed where we were going.'

'There was nothing I could do to prevent that. He may have known where to look for us. In any case there could have been no question of landing at Rasal, or even finding the place, in the middle of a sand-storm.'

'And what are we to do?'

'Sit here until the storm has passed on – unless you feel like going for a walk.'

'Don't be impertinent.'

'Then don't ask such damn silly questions.'

'How long are we likely to be stuck here?'

'I'd have thought you had had more experience of this sort of thing than I have. If we're lucky the storm might last only an hour or two. That depends on the speed it's travelling. But I have known a *haboob* to last for a couple of days.'

'If this one lasts only two hours it will be dark before we can move on.'

'Move! We shall have to wait for the dust to settle. We shall do well to get away from here by dawn. To start with, even if the sand hasn't bogged us down, I shall want to see how much room we have to get off. At present I have no idea. Secondly, I'm not starting the engines while there's any quantity of sand in the air. As I've already said, engines and sand don't go together. Sand means friction. Friction means heat. Heat means fire. You'll have to leave things to my judgement. Anyone who is expecting us at Rasal will have to wait, and that's all there is to it. I'm no miracle worker. The storm came from the direction of Rasal, so the people there will realise why we haven't shown up. We're lucky in this respect. Had we started later and run into this in the dark – well, use your imagination. Excuse me while I wash the grit out of my teeth.' Biggles had to talk at the top of his voice to make himself heard.

He opened a bottle of soda-water, drank the contents slowly and rejoined Bertie in the cockpit.

By now, with a hideous brown fog roaring past outside, it was almost dark. The noise as the wind screamed and howled, snatching at the aircraft, was like the end of the world. Scraps of debris that may have been twigs torn from bushes or even small pebbles, struck the wind-screen like bullets. Fine sand found its way inside, although joints were fitted as tightly as precision crafts-manship could make them.

'How did Zorlan take it?' asked Bertie.

'He's disgruntled by this hitch in his arrangements, but he got no change out of me. Something in his manner has always rubbed my hair the wrong way; now he's beginning to annoy me. I can understand him being dead set on his job. I'm a bit like that myself. But there's more behind it than seems natural. You'd never really know him. He's as deep as the ocean. He gives me a feeling that what he's saying isn't always what he's thinking. No matter. Go inside and get yourself a drink. There's no hurry. We're going to be here for some time.'

CHAPTER 8

RASAL AL SHARAB

FOR the next six hours conditions in the cabin of the Merlin were anything but comfortable. The lights, run off a battery, were still functioning, but in a haze of fine dust that had found its way in they showed only as a murky yellow glow.

For most of the time an embarrassing silence reigned, although of course the noise outside was considerable, gusts of sand-landen wind causing the aircraft to shudder. Zorlan still behaved as though in some way Biggles was responsible for their predicament. He did not speak, even when Ginger handed round some food and drink. Once Ginger tried to ease the tension by making a remark on a humorous note, but finding it fell flat he did not persist. After the refreshments Biggles and Bertie returned to the cockpit where the social atmosphere was less depressing.

That was the only advantage gained. Outside the *haboob* raged as if determined to strip the surface off the desert; and from the noise made by the sand as it lashed the aircraft it seemed to be succeeding. Dust, mostly so fine as to be invisible, found a way in to worry the eyes, nose and nostrils. It grated between the teeth. There was nothing unusual in this. Such storms have always been a feature of desert countries. An Arab caught in the open knows what to do. His only chance of survival is to make his camel kneel and with his head wrapped up crouch close beside it on the leeward side.

It was about midnight when Bertie remarked he thought the worst was over. The wind was less violent and instead of being constant came in fitful gusts. An hour later there was no doubt about it. The gusts came in less frequent intervals. The centre of the storm had gone on its way, leaving the atmosphere as thick with dust as a fog that hangs over London on a November day.

Biggles' biggest worry was the quantity of sand that might have been piled up against the aircraft; particularly the wheels, for if they had been buried, without tools to dig them out, to get them clear would present a problem. After a while, in his anxiety to know the worst he took a torch, and covering the lower part of his face with a towel went out to investigate.

He was soon back. 'Not too bad,' he reported with relief in his voice. 'There's less sand round the wheels than I would have supposed. I can only imagine that the wind was strong enough to carry most of the stuff right over the *wadi*. Those thorn bushes in front of us may have acted as a break and stopped a lot of it. The fact that we were dead in line with the wind would make a difference, too. When we start the engines the slipstream should blow away any loose stuff. It's no use thinking yet about taking off. Another couple of hours should make a lot of difference. Whatever Zorlan may think about it I'm taking no chances to oblige him. I'll decide when to go.'

Bertie looked through the glass panel. 'They all seem to have gone to sleep.'

'Good. That saves any argument.'

Time crawled on. Three, four, five o'clock ticked up on the instrument panel. Bertie had gone to sleep. Biggles, conscious of what depended on him, could only doze uneasily.

From one of these naps, which must have been longer than usual, he awoke with a start to find a sickly khaki-tinted dawn creeping through the wind-screen. Looking through the side window towards the east, he saw the sun showing its face, a dull orange monstrosity, bloated and distorted by the veil of dust that still hung in the air. But the great thing was that he could see it at all, for that meant within a short time the atmosphere should not be too thick for flying the short distance he had to go.

He poked Bertie in the ribs. 'It's daylight. Time to get mobile. Tell Ginger to get cracking with some coffee. My mouth's like the bottom of a bird-cage.'

He went out and examined the state of the machine, starting at the wheels. He was satisfied to find they were buried only as far up as the axles, and he had no difficulty in clearing this with his hands. The rest of the machine appeared to have suffered no damage. He next surveyed the landscape, such as it was. He saw he was right about the acacia scrub acting as a break, for it was more than half buried in a dune that had formed. This was directly in the way of any forward movement, but as the ground beyond was clear it would only be necessary to turn the aircraft and take up a line that would miss it. The floor of the *wadi* had been swept flat, without an obstruction of any sort. Indeed, the surface was a little too flat for his peace of mind. The question was, how soft was it?

He walked a little way on it dragging his feet. As he

suspected it was little more than dust deposited by the
storm; but he did not think it would be deep enough to
clog his wheels and so prevent the plane from gathering
the speed required to get off – a fate that has overtaken
more than one aircraft, and other wheeled vehicles for
that matter, in the desert. This was something that could
only be established by trial.*

Visibility was roughly a hundred yards but improving
steadily as the dust still in suspension settled and the
rays of the rising sun cut through it. He pulled out the
pieces of shirt that had protected the engines and returned to his seat.

Bertie handed him a cup of coffee and offered a plate
of biscuits. 'Well, how do things look?' he queried.

'I think we should be all right. You might tell Zorlan I
reckon to move off in about half an hour. Visibility will
have improved and I shall have time for a cigarette after
my breakfast. These biscuits would go down better if
there was a little less grit on 'em. But we mustn't expect
too much. If I know anything we shall be biting on dirt
for some time. Don't talk to me about the romance of
the desert.'

When the allotted time had passed and those in the
cabin had been warned to fasten their safety belts,
Biggles made ready to take off. 'I shall let the engines
run for a bit to blow away any loose stuff,' he told
Bertie. 'You keep an eye on the sky. It wouldn't surprise

---

* Desert sand is unpredictable from its appearance, as Biggles was
well aware, its degree of firmness or otherwise depending on the way
the grains of sand have fallen. These can pack down as hard as a
stone pavement or form a treacherous surface as soft as deep mud.
It was for this reason that in Iraq and similar overseas stations
service vehicles carried rolls of wire netting to help them to get
clear should they become stuck. *Author.*

me if a MIG slipped over to see if we were still about.'

To his great satisfaction the engines sprang to life at the first time of asking. He allowed them to tick over for a few minutes and then slowly ran them up to nearly full revs. Content to see from the instruments that they were doing what was expected of them, as soon as the machine started to move forward he throttled back.

'Okay,' said Bertie. 'Not a sign of anyone.'

'Fine.' The aircraft hung for a moment or two when Biggles tried to move it, but a little extra throttle, cautiously applied in case the machine showed signs of tipping up, did the trick. The wheels, with a slight jerk forward quickly checked, were clear. After that it was a fairly simple matter to manoeuvre into a position with a clear run forward, anyhow for as far as the still poor visibility allowed.

Biggles waited for the dust he himself had raised to settle. The crucial moment had come. If the soft sand clung to the wheels like deep mud or snow, as it might, anything could happen. The aircraft might end up stuck without hope of ever getting off. Too much throttle in an effort to reach flying speed might put it on its nose. A long run might find it confronted by an obstruction it could not clear and which in the poor visibility had been out of sight. It would have taken too long to explore the full length of the *wadi*. Not that it would have made much difference. The machine could not remain where it was. In short, everything depended on the next minute, possibly the lives of everyone in the plane.

In the event everything went as well as could be expected. The machine was slow picking up flying speed as was bound to be the case. The tail ploughed. Tense, eyes staring ahead, Biggles nursed the engines, not

daring to give them full throttle too quickly. He felt the
tail lift. Relieved of the dragging weight the aircraft
responded with a spurt, and just as all seemed well
danger appeared ahead in the form of an outcrop of
rock exposed by erosion. There was no question of stop-
ping. To swerve while the wheels were still running
through soft sand could only end in disaster; for the
wheels are designed to turn forward, and with the full
weight of the aircraft on them any departure from a true
line would almost certainly tear them off. There was
only one thing to do and Biggles did it. He gave the
engines everything and slowly but firmly pulled back the
control column. Vibrations ceased as the wheels 'un-
stuck'. They cleared the top of the grey peril, that lay
like a gigantic crocodile across the track, by inches.

Bertie put down his legs which he had lifted to his
chin to prevent them from being trapped had the machine crashed. He wiped imaginary sweat from his face.
It had lost some of its colour. 'Don't let's have any more
of that, old boy,' he pleaded with intense feeling. 'I can't
take it.'

Biggles smiled wanly. 'Neither can I. When I was
younger I could laugh at close squeaks – but not now.
They aren't funny any more. Keep an eye topsides for
MIGs. Ten minutes should see us at Rasal.'

This proved correct. Before them, from a place where
the *wadi* widened before breaking down altogether, extensive groves of date palms soared up to burst like
clouds of green feathers. Beyond them on a slight slope
clustered a conglomeration of small, square, mud-brick
houses which, with flat roofs, looked like so many
boxes. All were studded with tiny black holes which
apparently were unglazed windows. Conspicuously

standing apart, from above a castellated wall rose a larger building surmounted by a dome.

'This must be it,' said Biggles. 'Better confirm with Zorlan before I go down.'

Bertie made the inquiry. 'Right,' he advised. 'This is Rasal. Zorlan says go down wherever you can find room, but make it as close to the town as possible.'

Biggles made two circuits studying the ground. Then, having chosen what he decided was the best place, he landed beside a long plantation and ended his run as close as he could get to the trees, partly to take advantage of any shade they might give, but more particularly to reduce the risk of being seen from above. He switched off, got out, lit a cigarette and returned the stares of several men who had appeared from within the dark recesses of the plantation.

Zorlan emerged from the cabin with the two bodyguards, as usual carrying his portfolio. 'Wait,' he ordered. 'I shall return as soon as I can get away, although if I am offered hospitality I couldn't decline it without giving offence – you understand.'

'I take it we shall be all right here?' queried Biggles dubiously. 'I mean, the local lads won't come out with knives to carve us up? I seem to recall that these desert warriors have little time for strangers, particularly infidels like us,'

'You will be quite safe. I feel sure that the sultan will have given orders that you are not to be molested.'

'I hope you're right. When you come back you'll bring another passenger with you? Is that the idea?'

'That is the intention.' Zorlan walked away followed closely by the two guards.

Biggles drew on his cigarette with satisfaction. 'Well,

at least we've managed to get here. I'm nothing for exploring, so I suggest we make ourselves comfortable in the cabin and have an early lunch in comfort. On this crazy jaunt it's obviously wise to eat when you can.'

The others agreed.

'I wonder what sort of passenger Zorlan will pull out of the bag for us this time,' said Ginger as they went inside.

'Nothing would surprise me,' rejoined Biggles – an assertion he was later to recall and withdraw. 'I must say I find this hanging about, always waiting for something or somebody, more than a little tiresome. Patience isn't my long suit. When I've got a job to do I like to get on with it.'

Thereafter they passed the time by enjoying a substantial meal, now overdue. A small crowd had gathered on the fringe of the plantation, apparently from idle curiosity, but none came near the plane. The air continued to clear as the dust raised by the storm fell slowly back to earth. It became hotter as the sun flamed its eternal course across the cloudless heavens.

'What do you suppose Zorlan is doing all this time?' muttered Bertie irritably, after a long spell of silence during which Biggles had lowered his stock of cigarettes.

'Probably arguing about some clause or trying to get the sultan's signature on one of the documents he's carrying, I imagine,' answered Biggles moodily. 'If he's squatting with the sultan round the usual dish, scooping up boiled mutton and rice with his fingers, he's welcome to it. Before we left home I was more or less given to understand that the purpose behind the expedition was to organise a hook-up, some sort of agreement, between Zarat and Rasal. I have a feeling the negotiations have struck a snag. There's nothing unusual about that. I've never heard of negotiations that didn't strike one. I was told nothing about oil coming into the picture, although the Air Commodore must have known about it. Perhaps he thought there was no need to mention it. As I see the whole thing now oil lies at the root of it. Just where it is I don't know and I don't care. No doubt an agreement between these two countries is thought desirable, but an oil concession, and that is what I now suspect Zorlan has been sent here to get, puts a very different complexion on the business. Oil is liquid gold. It makes millionaires faster than anything else on earth. Where there's oil, trouble is never far away. To me, when I think of the lives it costs, the stuff stinks.'

'But whoever makes the millions it won't be us,' sighed Bertie.

'You're dead right. It will not.'

'It'd be interesting to know what Zorlan is getting out of it,' put in Ginger.

'You can be quite sure of one thing. It won't be peanuts.'

Ginger walked to the door to survey the scene outside. 'Hey! Come and take a dekko at what's coming,' he invited.

'Coming here?'

'It's coming this way.'

'What is?'

'It looks like a bit of a circus procession that's lost its way.'

Biggles and Bertie got up to investigate.

'Well, well,' murmured Bertie. 'This show gets

more and more like something out of the Arabian
Nights.'

Biggles did not comment. Lines furrowed his forehead in a frown of disapproval, if not anger.

The circus, as Ginger had described it, consisted
firstly of a camel, with extravagant trappings, from the
back of which rose a tall black object that looked rather
like a half-inflated balloon. Beside the beast, three on
each side, strode what, from the drawn scimitars they
carried on their shoulders, was an escort of half a dozen
men in uniforms that might have been copied from an
illuminated oriental manuscript. That was not all. In
front, looking ridiculous in Western clothes and carrying a modern portfolio, walked Zorlan between the two
Zarat bodyguards.

'It isn't true,' breathed Bertie, briskly polishing his
eyeglass.

'I wish you were right,' growled Biggles.

'What do you make of it?' questioned Ginger.

'So *this* is the passenger we've come to fetch,' sighed
Biggles. 'No wonder Zorlan was cagey about saying
who it was. A little while ago I said nothing would surprise me. I take it back. This knocks me backwards on
my haunches.'

'It must be a prince, at least,' offered Ginger.

'In this part of the world, no men, not even princes,
travel in those covered wagon affairs.'

'What, then?'

'It's a woman.'

'Great grief! For crying out loud! You don't say!'

'You'll see. Or more likely you won't see. There are
still men in the world, even in so-called civilised parts,
who object to any other male casting an eye on their

females. We've carried some queer freight in our time, but if this is the load we're to carry to Zarat it'll be top of the list.'

'But she can't get into the cabin in that paraphernalia.'

'You won't see any more of her when she gets out, if I know anything about it.'

The little procession came up and halted as near to the cabin door as it could get. The camel leader touched his animal on the leg with his wand. The creature 'couched' obediently. The curtains of the canopy were drawn and out stepped a slim figure swathed from head to foot in some fine black material. Not even an eye was showing.

Breathed Bertie: 'I'd like to see who . . .'

'Watch your step,' cut in Biggles. 'In Moslem country this sort of luggage can be more dangerous than high explosive.'

Zorlan came close to Biggles and whispered: 'Be very careful.'

'What is all this?' demanded Biggles.

'Our passenger, of course.'

'I'd already grasped that. Who is she?'

'The daughter of the Sultan of Rasal al Sharab.'

'And what are we supposed to do with her?'

'Deliver her safely to her affianced husband. I have just concluded a marriage contract between the Sultan of Rasal al Sharab and the Sheikh of Zarat. Take great care. The sultan thinks the world of his daughter.'

'So much that he'd sell her for a cut in the oil deal,' said Biggles dryly.

'That's no business of yours.'

'Any more surprises up your sleeve?'

'No. This should be all. Once the sheikh has signed the formal documents we shall be free to return home.'

'Isn't the sultan taking a chance to allow his precious daughter to be flown to Zarat in the present conditions?'

'Speed is all important.'

'For whom? You or the lady?' Biggles couldn't keep sarcasm out of his voice.

'Let us say for everybody.'

'Did you warn the sultan there were hostile aircraft about?'

'No. It seemed unnecessary to worry him unduly.'

'I like the word unduly,' retorted Biggles, tight-lipped. 'What are you trying to do? Push the responsibility on to me should anything go wrong?'

Zorlan did not answer.

'In fairness to the sultan, if not his daughter, you should have warned him of the risks,' challenged Biggles. 'It appears to me that for a political agent you seem mighty anxious to push this deal through, regardless.'

'Am I not taking the same risks myself?' inquired Zorlan frostily. 'Any delay now might undo the work of months.'

'All right. Let's not waste any more time arguing, but you might as well know how I feel about it. Let's get on,' concluded Biggles.

By now, under the guidance of Bertie and Ginger, the passenger had been ushered into her seat. Zorlan and the two bodyguards went in and took their places. Ginger made a signal to Biggles and closed the door from the inside.

'If we don't run into trouble we should just about make Suwara Oasis in daylight,' said Biggles to Bertie. 'I shall go flat out just above the carpet. Keep your eyes wide open. If anything should happen to the damsel we've had pushed on to us we shall make more enemies than friends, to say nothing of starting an international rumpus. I may be wrong, but I imagine that in an emergency the lass in the cabin will be as helpless as a day-old chick. I don't like it. However . . . let's go.'

Biggles started the engines, took a last look round the sky and taxied well away from the plantation.

'All clear,' reported Bertie.

The rhythmic purring of the engines rose to a roar and the Merlin raced across the arid ground, leaving a cloud of sand swirling high in its wake.

CHAPTER 9

THE TRUTH COMES OUT

For every minute that passed without incident on the run to Zarat, Biggles was thankful, knowing it reduced, if only by a little, the risk of interception. But he did not relax.

He had meant every word of what he had said before the start. Aside from the natural anxiety of having a woman in his care, he realised he was engaged on a mission fraught with appalling possibilities should it fail. In view of what he now knew he became more and more convinced that the Air Commodore had under-estimated the dangers. Perhaps through ignorance. Indeed, the whole business was more complex than he could have anticipated or he would have had more to say about the details. Had something gone wrong? Had an unknown factor arisen to complicate matters? Biggles wondered.

Failure for any reason would mean questions from more than one source. What was a British aircraft doing in that part of the world? Who had sent it there? For what purpose? If the female passenger was killed or even injured every Middle-Eastern potentate would blame the British Government for allowing it to happen. The responsibility for seeing that nothing of the sort did happen now rested on his shoulders. There could be no excuses.

He flew on full throttle, his eyes never resting from their scrutiny of the sky, section by section – or as much of it as he could see. He was never more than fifty feet above the ground, so that ruled out danger from below, unless a wandering Arab took a pot shot at them. He was not worried about that. The chances of such a man scoring a hit in a vital spot, or even of hitting the machine at all, were negligible. Bertie did in fact call attention to two horsemen galloping southward, but they did not stop as the plane roared over their heads.

The hot air was choppy, as he knew it would be, but the very speed at which the Merlin was travelling did much to iron out the bumps. It cut through them like an arrow.

The *wadi* had petered out into open *sabkha* and with three-quarters of the distance to the oasis behind them he began to breathe more freely. The sky ahead was still as clear as a newly-painted ceiling, without a speck on it. To the left the sun was hanging low, like an enormous orange, over the horizon, but already the day was dying in the golden glow which in desert countries seems to soak into everything, including the air itself. An almost intangible smudge with a ragged top crept over the edge of the world in front of the machine.

'We've done it,' said Bertie jubilantly. 'There's the oasis.'

'Keep your fingers crossed,' requested Biggles cautiously. 'We aren't there yet.'

However, the oasis quickly hardened into something more solid and in a few more minutes the aircraft was making a circuit round it. Not a soul could be seen.

Beneath the palms everything was darkly vague in the failing daylight.

Biggles, having completed his circuit, had brought the plane round to where he had landed on the previous occasion and was gliding in to land when a rocket soared from somewhere among the palms to burst in a shower of crimson sparks. It was followed by another; but even before this one had discharged its warning signals Biggles had opened up and turned away.

'We were patting ourselves on the back too soon,' he rasped viciously. 'Tell Zorlan someone is firing red rockets from the oasis. Ask him what he wants me to do.'

Bertie went through the door. He was back within a minute. 'He says make for Quarda.'

'And land there?'

'Presumably.'

'Has he any idea of what could have · happened here?'

'If he has he didn't tell me. He looked damned annoyed.'

'I thought the going was too easy to be true,' muttered Biggles as he pulled the machine round and took up the course for the ruins. 'This is becoming fantastic. What on earth are we going to do with a *bint** who isn't allowed to uncover her face? As if we hadn't got enough on our plate without her.'

'We only need to find rockets waiting for us at Quarda and we shall be up the creek good and proper,' remarked Bertie lugubriously.

'Something seems to be cooking in that direction, anyway,' returned Biggles. 'Look below.'

---

* *Bint*, Arabic for girl. Common service slang in the Middle East.

Roughly five miles short of the ruins, galloping across the wilderness in the same direction as themselves, casting incredibly long shadows in the setting sun, was a little knot of horsemen. In different circumstances they would have made a wild, thrilling spectacle.

'Whoever they are we shall be there first,' observed Bertie optimistically.

'A fat lot of good that'll do us if they turn out to be some of Alfondari's mob armed with rifles.'

'In which case we shan't get much blanket-drill* tonight.'

They reached the oasis. Biggles flew round it and across it several times before, seeing no movement, he put down his wheels and landed close by the discarded camouflage used on their earlier visit. For a minute or two he left the engines running while he surveyed the ruin-littered hill. Then he switched off and got down just as Zorlan and Ginger emerged from the cabin.

'Well, here we are. Now what about it?' inquired Biggles.

'Something must have happened either at Suwara or the sheikh's palace in Zarana.'

'That's pretty obvious unless some fool imagines it's Guy Fawkes day. It seems we can't move without something happening somewhere.'

'No doubt the sheikh will get in touch with us.'

'Does he know we've got a present on board for him?'

'Of course.'

'And if we couldn't land her at Suwara we were to bring her here?'

'That was the arrangement.'

* *Blanket-drill.* R.A.F. slang for sleep.

'So the sheikh thought there might be trouble?'

'He was prepared for it.'

'We overtook some riders coming this way. They were travelling fast.'

'That might be the sheikh, or some of his men bringing a message.'

'What are you going to do with the lady?'

'For the time being she will have to stay where she is, in the cabin.'

'These men coming here might be enemies. Wouldn't it be better to take her on to Ankara, where she would be safe?'

'No. That wouldn't do at all. I'm not letting her out of my sight.'

Biggles shrugged. 'All right. Have it your way. You know best.'

'All we can do for the moment is wait here for news.'

'And if these horsemen on the way here turn out to be enemies?'

'There should be time enough for you to fly off and take the lady back to her father. It would be a tragedy, but it would be better than having her captured.'

'Very well. But I shall have to remind you of a detail you may have overlooked. To make it go an aeroplane needs petrol. We started with plenty, enough for our estimated needs and a fair margin; but at the rate we're using it we shan't be able to go on much longer.'

'It may not be necessary.'

'I trust you're right. As you're in charge of the lady you'd better stay with her. I'll go up to higher ground to see if there is any sign of the men we passed on the way here. They must have seen us, but they may not know we landed here.'

'I agree, but don't go far away in case it becomes necessary to make a quick take-off.'

'My friends are as capable of flying the machine as I am.' Biggles turned to Bertie and Ginger. 'Stand fast and be ready to move in a hurry. I'll be back.' So saying he walked quickly up the hill.

The sun had set and dusk had dimmed the scene, but there was still enough twilight to give a fair view over the flat landscape. Reaching a point that overlooked the right direction, Biggles stopped to look and saw that he was only just in time. The horsemen, six of them, were closer than he had supposed they would be. Standing still, he waited for them to come nearer, and within a short time was gratified to observe that the sheikh, easily recognisable by his red tunic, was there, leading the party. Reaching the nearest palms, everyone dismounted.

Biggles walked forward, showing himself, instantly to be covered by five rifles. He raised his hands high and continued to walk on. The sheikh said something to his men and advanced to meet him. The rifles were lowered.

When the sheikh came up, somewhat to Biggles' surprise he offered a coffee-coloured hand, as small and neat as a woman's. 'So you have arrived safely,' he greeted in a soft pleasing voice, in perfect English.

'Yes, sir. We saw rockets at Suwara so we came on here. I trust the trouble isn't serious.'

'No. A cousin of mine, acting for people of a different political persuasion, tried to start a revolution in order to usurp my position. I had prepared for something of the sort and in any case he misjudged the loyalty of my people. It is all over or I should not be here. A few rebels fled to Suwara where they are now being rounded up. As it would not have been entirely safe for you to land there, I left for Quarda, having given orders that rockets should be fired if the plane attempted to land.' The sheikh studied Biggles' face. 'You brought back what you went to fetch?'

'Yes, sir.'

'Where is the plane now?'

'Just over the hill. I will take you to it and accept your orders for what you wish to be done.'

'You are in charge of it?'

'I am.'

'You are an Englishman?'

'I am.'

'Employed officially by your government?'

'Indirectly. I am an officer of the air police service.'

'Do you know what all this is about?'

'I know more now than I did when I started. I was not fully informed, although that may have been the result of unforeseen circumstances. My orders were simply to fly Professor Zorlan here. I was told to take further instructions from him; but as captain of the aircraft, how it is employed is my responsibility. I have two assistant pilots with me able to take over should it be necessary.'

'Quite so. Come over here. I would like you if you will, or if you can, to answer one or two questions for me.' The sheikh took Biggles by the arm and drew him into the deep gloom under some palms. 'How well do you know this man Professor Zorlan?' he inquired when they had halted.

'Well,' answered Biggles, taken slightly off guard by the unexpectedness of the question, 'I can't really say that I know him at all. I had never seen him, or heard of him, until I was ordered to bring him here.'

'Now, having seen something of him, what impression have you formed?'

'I find that a difficult question to answer.'

'Which I take to mean you don't like him,' came back the sheikh, shrewdly.

'It isn't for me to criticise a man appointed by a superior authority. What I think personally doesn't enter into it.'

'Let us put it like this. Have you had any reason to doubt his integrity?'

'Not his integrity. His methods perhaps. We have clashed on those. You must have a reason for asking such a question.'

The sheikh hesitated – a long pause with his eyes searching Biggles' face. 'I am going to take you into my confidence,' he went on. 'You know that oil has been located in Zarat?'

'Since I came here I have heard it has been discovered in the region, but until this moment I didn't know exactly where.'

'Professor Zorlan, acting on behalf of the British Government, had two objects in coming here. The first was to bring about an alliance between myself and my neighbour the Sultan of Rasal al Sharab.'

'That is what I understood.'

'The pact, according to our custom, is to be strengthened by my marriage to the sultan's daughter, who is now here.'

'That is what I had imagined since my visit to Rasal al Sharab.'

'Professor Zorlan's second undertaking, not unconnected with the first, was to obtain from me a concession for the exploitation of the oil, chiefly to prevent it from falling into other hands. I could not from my own slim treasury finance such a project.'

'I had surmised that.'

'Professor Zorlan brought with him certain documents prepared by your government which I was requested to sign in order that there should be a written record of the transaction.'

'Naturally. That is understandable.'

'So I would agree. The papers are in order and with one exception I have signed them. The exception is a document, detached from the rest, the purport of which I find hard to believe. I am, or I try to be, a man of honour, and if I did sign it I would have to stand by it. But I tell you frankly that I am amazed your government should send to me such a contract for signature. The contents came as a complete surprise, and I feel that before I put my name to it I should obtain confirmation.'

Biggles was looking puzzled. 'What is this document?'

'It gives Professor Zorlan, personally, for his services, seven per cent of all the money that accrues from the sale of the oil.'

Biggles' jaw dropped. For a few seconds he could only stare, speechless. '*How* much did you say?' he asked incredulously.

'Seven per cent.'

'For his own private pocket?'

'Yes.'

'That would soon make him several times a millionaire.'

'Of course.'

Biggles drew a deep breath as understanding poured in to what had been a void. Zorlan's behaviour was now explained – his anxiety, his demand for urgency, his close guard on his portfolio, his unscrupulous attitude ... 'Don't sign that paper, sir,' he advised trenchantly.

'You don't think it's genuine?'

'I can't believe the British Government would ever issue such an extraordinary demand. Moreover, had it done so the clause would have been incorporated in the general contract and not, as you say, on a loose sheet.'

'That is what I thought. If what we believe is correct it can only mean that Zorlan must himself have composed this document and included it with the others.'

'That's how it looks to me, sir.'

'But how are we to prove it?'

'If you challenge him with it he will of course deny it.'

'Exactly. But what if it should be genuine? I would not like your government to think I was going back on my word. I promised that if the appropriate documents were sent to me I would sign them.'

'Weren't you shown a draft agreement?'

'No. You see, the negotiations were conducted by my younger brother, who is my representative in London.'

'Leave this to me,' requested Biggles. 'It won't take me long to get it sorted out. A delay of a few hours can make no difference. You say you have signed the other papers, those relating to the oil concession and the pact with the Sultan of Rasal al Sharab?'

'Yes. And as you have been to Rasal al Sharab no

doubt the sultan, who I know very well, will have signed them, too. What shall I tell Professor Zorlan to account for my withholding my signature from the one that refers to him?'

'I wouldn't even discuss it with him. You are within your rights in refraining from signing anything until you are satisfied with its authenticity.'

'I suspect he could be a dangerous man if thwarted.'

'I'm quite sure of it.'

'What will you do?'

'Get a message through to London.'

'How? I have no radio station here.'

'I have a plane.'

'It would be some time getting to London and back.'

'It might not be necessary to go as far as London. One of my pilots could get on the telephone from Ankara. No, on second thoughts not Ankara. There are too many prying eyes and ears there. We have discovered that already. The aircraft would have to refuel, so it would be on the ground for some time. Athens would be better. Or possibly Cyprus, where there is a Royal Air Force station. I'll decide when I've checked how much petrol we have. From Athens my assistant pilot could speak direct to my chief in London.'

'This will take time.'

'We have a fast plane and without intermediate stops it should be back here easily by dawn tomorrow. A modern plane can cover a lot of ground in twelve hours. But as it can't be in two places at once, the question arises, which do you consider the more urgent: to take your fiancée home or send the plane immediately to

Athens, if we have enough petrol for the trip without refuelling. Either way it would be safer to fly by night than in daylight. Hostile aircraft are in the vicinity and we have already been attacked.'

'By far the most important thing is to settle this question of Zorlan's personal document. Everything else can wait, so I would say send the plane off at once. Do I understand you would remain here?'

'That is my intention. The crux of the situation is here.'

'That would suit me admirably.'

'For any particular reason?'

'I feel I can rely on you to deal with any emergency that might arise during my absence.'

Biggles' eyebrows went up. 'Your absence – where?'

'It is time I returned to Zarana, my capital, and showed my face to my people to maintain their confidence. Order has been restored, but it might be dangerous for me to be away too long. If there is any trouble still simmering it could break out again were I not there.'

'But what about our lady passenger? She is in the cabin of the aircraft. She can't remain there if it is to leave.'

'She must wait here. She will be safe with you. Tomorrow, as early as possible, I shall return for her and take her to my palace. I shall take two men with me. The other three can remain. That will give you a force of five of my men should trouble occur. It should be enough.'

'But your horses must be tired?'

'Not too tired. It is an easy journey. They are being

watered. After a rest they will be all right. They are used to long journeys.'

'Very well, sheikh. If that is how you want it I have nothing more to say.'

At this juncture a voice could be heard calling.

'That's Zorlan,' said Biggles. 'No doubt he's wondering what I'm doing. We'd better go.'

'Will you tell him what we have planned?'

'No. Definitely.'

Leaving two men watering the horses from the skin bags they carried, everyone else walked down the hill to the plane. Zorlan had come forward a little way. He looked at Biggles suspiciously. 'So it was the sheikh.'

'As you see.'

'You were a long time.'

'He's been telling me about what happened in the capital, Zarana.'

'What did happen?'

'Apparently a cousin, working for other interests, tried to seize power; but the coup failed.'

'And what is the plan now?'

'The sheikh thinks it would be advisable for him to return home to let his people see all is well. He is leaving three men here to help us in case of trouble. With the original two guards that will make five.'

'Why did he come here?'

'Ask him yourself. I imagine he would be anxious to know if we had brought his future wife; also to let us know why we could not land at Suwara Oasis.'

'What about the woman? Is he leaving her here?'

'Yes.'

'Why?'

'I'm not a thought-reader. He may have decided that a

thirty-mile ride on horseback to the palace might be rather much. It might not be entirely safe there yet, anyway.'

'Wouldn't it have been better to fly her, if not to the palace, as far as Suwara, instead of leaving her all night in the aircraft?'

'She won't be all night in the aircraft.'

'Why not?'

'I'm sending it off to be refuelled. The tanks are getting low and it would be folly to risk running out of petrol in this sort of country.'

'Sending? Does that mean you are staying here?'

'Yes. My fellows are quite capable of doing what is necessary. Don't worry. The machine should be back here by tomorrow morning.'

'But why the hurry? Why fly by night?'

'You seem to have forgotten there are other aircraft not far away and they have already given us a demonstration of why they are here. I must remind you that the aircraft is my responsibility.'

'I see,' said Zorlan in a curious tone of voice.

Leaving him, Biggles walked to where the sheikh was standing. 'Would you mind asking the lady to leave the cabin, sir? I'm afraid she is not going to have a very comfortable night and I cannot entirely guarantee her privacy.'

'I will attend to it. My men are building a palm-frond shelter in which, providing the weather does not change, she will be able to keep warm and perhaps get some sleep. I personally am not so much concerned with her privacy; that is merely a matter of conforming to traditional custom. The men will remain on guard.'

'Won't she need some refreshment?'

'If you have anything . . .'

'When I have briefed my pilots I'll bring something
from our stores. Excuse me.' Biggles walked to where
Bertie and Ginger were watching the proceedings.
'Come over here, I want to talk to you,' he said
quietly.

CHAPTER 10

ZORLAN MAKES AN OFFER

HAVING taken Bertie and Ginger to a distance where there was no risk of being overheard, Biggles spoke seriously. 'Listen carefully. There's some monkey business going on. When we've checked up on petrol I want you two to go to Athens.'

'*Athens!*' Ginger's voice nearly cracked. 'What's this in aid of?' he asked, in his astonishment resorting to service slang.

'I've just been talking to the sheikh. He's not happy. There's reason to suppose that Zorlan is a crook – well, if not a crook he may be trying to pull a fast one.'

'How?'

'He's asking the sheikh to sign a paper giving him seven per cent of the oil revenue. He presented the document as if it was part of the official contract.'

'Seven per cent! Somebody must be out of his mind.'

'It isn't the sheikh. He's no fool. He smells a rat. So do I. So far he's refused to sign, but he's worried because he thinks there's just a remote chance of the document being genuine, in which case he'd hate our people to

121

accuse him of going back on his word. To be on the safe side he wants to check up before he signs away millions of pounds a year.'

'I should jolly well think so,' put in Bertie indignantly. 'Why not have it out with Zorlan here and now?'

'No, we can't do that simply on suspicion. We've no proof, no evidence, that he's playing his own game. That's what it would amount to if we were right. We've got to be sure. Now, this is the drill. The sheikh has had a bit of a revolution on his hands. He believes everything is now under control, but he wants to be certain before he takes his fiancée home. He's going, but all being well he's coming back for her in the morning.'

'Leaving her here for the night?'

'There's no alternative.'

'If Zorlan gets wind of what's going on aren't you afraid he might get up to some mischief?'

'No. What can he do? With the machine away he can't leave here. There will be five men to mount guard and he knows the sheikh will be back here early tomorrow morning. Leave that to me. The most urgent thing is to get confirmation or otherwise of this seven per cent racket. We can only get that from the Air Commodore, and the safest way would be by word of mouth. Any sort of signal, radio or cablegram, would be too dangerous. It might be seen or heard by too many people. You've got to get in touch with the chief by telephone.'

'But why Athens? Ankara, being nearer, would be quicker.'

Biggles shook his head. 'Too risky. Alfondari or some of his people might be there, watching for the plane to

come back. They'd never take their eyes off you. I did
consider Cyprus, but I'm not sure of the com-
munications there with London. Let's play safe and
make it Athens. I think we have enough petrol. When
you get there one of you can get the tanks topped up
while the other gets on the phone to the Yard. If the
chief has gone home get the operator to put you through
to him.'

'What exactly do you want us to say?'

'It's quite simple. Tell him that Zorlan is trying to get
the sheikh to sign a document, apparently official, giving
him seven per cent of the oil revenue. The sheikh is
suspicious, and we need hardly be surprised at that. Is
he to sign this paper? The answer I want from the chief
is a definite yes or no. It's as simple as that. Aim to get
back here by dawn. Don't go near Ankara or Istanbul
either way. If you're on course they'll be well to the
north of you. You're not likely to meet anything, so
until you're clear of Turkey I wouldn't show lights. And
don't answer ground signals if you're challenged. Press
on. You'll have to take a chance on that.'

'I'll work out the course in the cabin as soon as we get
started,' said Ginger.

'Right. I see the sheikh has unloaded our precious
passenger, so let's have a look at the petrol position.'

They went into the aircraft and were able to confirm
there was ample fuel for the journey plus a fair
margin.

'Okay,' said Biggles briskly. 'Get on with it. The
sooner you're away the better. One last thing. If by any
chance you get back here before daylight fire a red-to-
green recognition flare. I'll then light a fire clear of the
hill as a pin-point to touch down. That's all. Ginger, you

might hand me out a few bottles of soda water and one or two packets of biscuits.'

He got out. From the cabin door Ginger passed him the bottles and some light food. He waved and stepped back, then waited until the engines had been started and the machine taxied out. As it left the ground he turned to find the sheikh standing near him.

'Everything in order?' asked the sheikh.

'Yes sir. There should be no trouble.'

'Good. In that case I'll move off. I'm much obliged to you for your assistance. I hope to see you in the morning.'

'No trouble at all, sir. In the circumstances I could hardly do less. Before you go you might care to take these to your fiancée.' He passed two bottles, an opener and a packet of sweet biscuits.

'Thank you.' The sheikh walked away.

With the drone of the plane receding Biggles took his cigarettes from his pocket, strolled to the base of the hill and found a seat on a piece of fluted column carved by hands that had long gone back to dust. Automatically he lit a cigarette, the light flaring in the darkness that had now enfolded the weary land. Not a breath of air moved. Even the palms had stopped whispering. The heat was still oppressive, but relieved of its tormentor, the sun, it was bearable. Little could be seen, for the moon had not yet shown its face, and the stars, although becoming brighter, were still dim in a sky of purple velvet. The figures of the guards moved like funereal ghosts, making no sound on the soft drifted sand. He could not see Zorlan, or the palm shelter to which the sheikh had referred; but he had no need to, nor did he want to. There was no point in speaking to the guards, for he was sure they would not understand his language, and of course he could not speak theirs.

Still, he had plenty to think about, although as far as he could judge no cause – no immediate cause, anyhow – for worry. As he had said, at the moment it was hard to see what Zorlan could do, however suspicious he may have been made by the turn of events, without making his own position worse. That his suspicions had been aroused was fairly evident from the questions he had asked. He knew the sheikh had been talking to him and must be wondering how much had been said. He could hardly fail to be disturbed by the sudden decision to send the aircraft away for refuelling. He might not guess the real reason, but he would probably work it out that the one he had been given was an excuse. On the face of it there was nothing more for the machine to do at Zarat. Its task complete it could have returned home, so what was the point of sending it away to be refuelled?

Yes, Zorlan would not overlook that, pondered Biggles. A man of his intelligence would realise that something was going on of which he had been kept in ignorance. There was another angle to that. Why, if the aircraft had finished its work, as apparently it had, why hadn't Zorlan given the order to return to London? Why tarry in dangerous country if there was no need? Biggles knew the answer to that. Zorland had done what he had been sent to do. The official contracts had been completed both by Zarat and Rasal al Sharab; but the document with which he was most concerned, his guarantee of seven per cent, had not yet been signed. That was why he had said nothing about departure. Presumably he still hoped that he would be able to get the sheikh to write his name on the paper which, as far as he was concerned, was the vital part of the operation.

The big question that must be exercising his mind now, reasoned Biggles, was had the sheikh mentioned this? Looked at critically, Zorlan's scheme – always supposing it was his own idea for making an easy fortune – might well have succeeded. The reason why it had failed could be summed up in one word. Avarice. He had demanded too much. Had he been content with a smaller percentage, which would still have made him a rich man, he might have got away with it and the present situation would never have arisen. As it was, he had underestimated the sheikh's intelligence. The enormous reward demanded had aroused his suspicions and he had withheld his hand.

It seemed to Biggles, thinking the matter over, that Zorlan was now in the proverbial cleft stick. What could he do? Would he drop the whole idea and be satisfied with what he was to be paid for the job? After all, even though he might be discredited he had broken no law, so legal proceedings would not be taken against him. If they were the resultant scandal would do no one any good. Biggles did not think he would give in so easily. It was more likely he would try to use the one trump card he still held. In his portfolio were the legitimate contracts that had been signed by the sheikh and the sultan. The thought of these gave Biggles his one cause for anxiety. What would he do with them? Would he destroy them, thereby scuttling the ship, so to speak? Would he in his frustration try to sell them to a foreign power to whom they might be of value? That would have to be prevented at any cost.

But all this, soliloquised Biggles, stubbing the butt of his cigarette in the sand, depended on the report the aircraft had gone to fetch. Nothing could be done until it arrived, when the truth would be known.

The silvery glow that is the advance guard of the moon spread upwards from the horizon to cast an eerie light on the pitiless desert, as doubtless it had done since the beginning of time. Biggles, in a contemplative mood, brooded on how seldom, if ever, it had known anything but trouble. Since the dawn of history invading armies must have marched and countermarched over the spot where he now sat, men without mercy who slew everyone, man, woman or child, who fell into their hands. Wherever they marched, before them ran a wave of terror. So proud were some of them of their evil reputation that they recorded it engraved on stone. What men had not done storm and earthquake had. No wonder the land was a wilderness. Even now war clouds were never far away.

A figure approached. It was Zorlan. He came close and said: 'So here you are. Do you mind if I sit down for a minute?' Without waiting for an answer, he joined Biggles on the broken column.

Biggles was in no mood for conversation, but could find no excuse to protest. 'Did you want to say something?' he asked, lighting another cigarette, hoping Zorlan would take the hint and go away.

'Nothing in particular,' replied Zorlan suavely. 'I'm very sorry things have turned out like this.'

'Like what?'

'Well, this confusion and delay.'

'I'm not bothered. I take things as they come.'

After a short silence Zorlan went on: 'You must have a difficult job.'

'If I didn't like it I wouldn't be doing it.'

'I imagine the money must be good. If I'm not being too personal what do they pay you for a risky operation like this one?'

Biggles stiffened slightly as he sensed what was coming. 'I'm on a flat salary,' he informed, without changing his tone of voice, wondering how far Zorlan would go.

'But surely they pay you danger money for special assignments, such as this, for instance?'

'They do not. I take what comes along.'

'But that's disgraceful. No doubt from time to time you are able to make a little on the side?'

'That sort of money doesn't come my way.'

'For my part I expect to be paid in proportion to the value of my work. Take the present case, for example. Provided I bring it to a successful conclusion, I shall receive a sum of money which might take you a long while to earn.'

'Very nice for you. Is there any doubt about it not being successful?'

'Well, things have not gone as smoothly as I expected. I anticipated being on my way home by now.'

'What's the trouble?'

'The sheikh. I was provided with papers which he had undertaken to sign, but now at the last minute he is being awkward.'

'You mean – he hasn't yet signed?'

'Not everything.'

'Too bad. There's nothing I can do about it.'

'It struck me you might use your influence with him.'

'What leads you to suppose I have any influence?'

'He seems to have taken a liking to you.'

'And so?'

'It occurred to me that if you could induce him to put his name to the one outstanding document, we need waste no more time here. We could start for home as soon as the plane returns.'

'It makes no difference to me how long I stay here.'

'It might.'

'What do you mean by that?'

'I have made no secret that I shall collect a substantial reward for my services. The sheikh is coming back here in the morning. I have the papers. Every hour we spend here is dangerous. If you could hasten our departure by getting the sheikh to sign the final document I would make it worth your while.'

'What have you in mind?'

'Shall we say a hundred pounds?'

Biggles nearly laughed out loud. Here was a man playing for a stake of millions, yet unable to find it in his heart to offer a bribe of more than a paltry hundred pounds. However, he kept his reactions under control.

'No thank you,' he said. 'In the first place, the sheikh, having no reason to take my word for anything, would probably refuse to sign. Secondly, I have always made it a rule to keep out of political issues such as this. I'm employed to fly aeroplanes, not juggle with matters that are outside my official duties.'

'Would five hundred pounds tempt you?'

'No, it would not. When I make a rule I stick to it. Whatever you want from the sheikh you'll have to get yourself.'

Another long pause. 'Of course, his hand could always be forced,' said Zorlan reflectively.

T—E

'Forced? How?'

'We have a ready-made hostage here.'

'Hostage?' For a second Biggles did not cotton on. Then the penny dropped. 'You're not talking about the girl?' he exclaimed incredulously.

'Who else?'

'Great heavens, man! Are you out of your mind?'

Zorlan mumbled: 'I shall have to do something.'

'Well, I wouldn't try anything like that,' countered Biggles frigidly. 'With those guards handy you're liable to lose your head, and I mean that literally. I wouldn't stand for it, anyway. And now, if that's all you have to say, I'll try to get some sleep while things are quiet.'

Zorlan got up and without another word walked away.

With calculating eyes, Biggles watched him go. He had always known the man was unscrupulous, but not to the extent he had just revealed. Strangely, perhaps, it had never occurred to him that Zorlan might try to bribe him, and the fact that he had attemped to do so was an indication of the desperation to which he had been driven. Any lingering doubts Biggles may have had about the authenticity of the vital document – vital, that is, for Zorlan – were now banished.

One factor that puzzled him was, how could it have happened that a man of Zorlan's character had been entrusted with such an important mission? He had always supposed him to be a professional agent. Had he been mistaken? Was Zorlan in fact a private individual who had been chosen for his knowlege of the country and the local languages? It was even possible that he had plotted the whole thing from the beginning in the hope of making an easy fortune. Either way, it was now clear that he had a dishonest streak in his make-up. What he was trying to do was inexcusable, for it could wreck the plans of the people who had trusted him and were apparently paying him well for his errand. What he had just proposed might even start a war between friendly nations.

With such sombre thoughts to occupy his mind, Biggles made his way to the spot where he had previously slept and settled down to pass the night as comfortably as circumstances permitted.

Sleep did not come easily. After what Zorlan had just said, he was less confident about the immediate future than he had been. He wondered how far the man would go to secure the fortune he had plotted to get. Thwarted, angry and desperate, now that he saw the probability of it slipping from his grasp, there might be no limit to his villainy.

CHAPTER 11

BIGGLES GETS TOUGH

BIGGLES did not sleep well. Lying on his back gazing at the stars, it was a long time before he went to sleep at all, and then for a while slumber was light and intermittent. Odd memories recurred to him, as so often happens in a wakeful night. The strange remark Alfondari had made when he had taken his pistol from him. Speaking of Zorlan, what was it he had said? 'He's only on one side – his own.' Or something to that effect. It now seemed that he had been right. Had this vague warning been mere guesswork, a shot in the dark, or had he known something? It was no use wondering about that now, but it was a disturbing thought.

Towards dawn, when he had dropped off to sleep more heavily, he was awakened by the penetrating cold that chilled his very bones. As it was futile to try to sleep in such conditions he sat up, and looking at his watch saw that it was nearly five o'clock. He lit a cigarette and settled down to wait for whatever sunrise might bring. Looking around in the now failing moonlight, he located the position of the palm-shelter by two guards who stood like statues, hands resting on the muzzles of their rifles, the butts on the ground. He could not see Zorlan. Apparently he had withdrawn to some corner of his own.

132

Squatting hunched up, he listened impatiently for the first sounds of the returning aircraft. Unshaven, teeth unbrushed, hair uncombed, feeling generally scruffy, he wished he had removed his toilet things from the machine. At the time of its departure it had not seemed important.

His satisfaction was therefore great when before very long, with the stars dying one by one, a distant drone reached his ears. It came nearer. His eyes searched the sky in the direction from which it was approaching, but he could see nothing. Not that he expected to, because it seemed unlikely the Merlin would be showing navigation lights. Collecting some dry palm fronds ready to light a fire, he waited for the recognition signal that had been arranged. It did not come. Breaking off from what he was doing, he stared upward, frowning, suddenly conscious of misgivings. The aircraft was not losing height, as was to be expected. The drone remained constant, passing directly overhead. With something of a shock he realised the engines were not those of the Merlin. They had a deeper beat. They were certainly not jets, so MIGs could be ruled out. What, then? The drone began to recede.

Baffled and disappointed, Biggles walked to his broken column to think the matter over. All he could be sure of was the undeniable fact that a plane, a heavy type, had passed overhead. What it was doing there or where it could be going so far from any regular route he could not imagine. There was no reason to suppose that its business had anything to do with him; but as it was not showing lights, which was significant, he could not shake off an uneasy feeling that it was in some way involved in the affairs of Zarat.

He was not surprised when Zorlan appeared and asked sharply: 'Why hasn't the plane landed?'

'The plane you heard was not ours,' answered Biggles.

'Are you sure of that?'

'Quite sure.'

'How can you be sure?'

'It happens that my job is aviation.'

'If the plane was not ours what do you suppose it was and what could it be doing here?'

'I haven't the remotest idea. Your guess would be as good as mine. We've already had proof that my machine is not the only one operating in the district.'

'Could it have been a MIG?'

'No. I can assure you of that.'

Zorlan said no more. He waited for a minute or two and then strode away.

Biggles was content to see him go. He was not in the mood for questions. He fetched and drank a bottle of soda water, munching a biscuit with it.

The sky was now lightening in the first rays of a colourful dawn and it was not long before he heard the sound he so anxiously awaited. This time there was no mistake. It was the Merlin. It came on, losing height, wheels down, to circle the hill before making a good landing. As it taxied to its old position Biggles walked to meet it. The engines died. Bertie stepped down.

'How did you get on?' asked Biggles tersely, as Ginger joined them.

'All right. No trouble, no trouble at all, old boy. Tanks topped up. I spoke to the Air Commodore. Told him the lot. Took a bit of time. He had to speak to someone else.'

'What did he say? Out with it.'

'You were right – all along the line. Zorlan has no
authority whatsoever to ask the sheikh to sign anything
except the official documents that were handed to him in
London. There was nothing in them about him getting a
share of the oil, or anything else. When I mentioned
seven per cent the chief nearly choked. Zorlan did the
job for a fee. He's had half of it. The arrangement was
the other half would be paid when he got back.'

'Did the chief say what I'm to do?'

'He certainly did – and how. You're to take charge,
relieving Zorlan of all the papers. Please yourself about
how you do it. Use your initiative about how you get
home with them.'

'Is that all?'

'Practically. He suggested it would be a good thing to
burn the paper about the seven per cent to make sure it
doesn't fall into wrong hands.'

'Did you tell him the others had been signed?'

'I said I thought so. Naturally we hadn't seen them;
but you'd spoken to the sheikh and we'd also been to
Rasal al Sharab.'

'Good. Thanks, Bertie. You've done a good job. Now
we know just how we stand. Was anything said about
what we were to do with Zorlan?'

'No. I imagine it's supposed we shall bring him home
with us to collect the other half of his commission.
Nothing was said about cancelling it. We couldn't very
well leave him stranded here.'

Biggles looked dubious. 'The sheikh may have something to say about that when he learns that Zorlan tried
to work a swindle on him.'

'Do you have to tell him?'

'He's bound to ask; and we can't push off without another word with him. He may be relying on us to fly his fiancée to Suwara. He said he'd be back early, so we can expect him any time now. If he doesn't want us for anything there's no reason why we shouldn't head for home.'

'He must have spent most of the night in the saddle.'

'That's his affair. He appeared to see no difficulty about it. By the way, did you see or hear anything of another aircraft near here?'

'No. Why?'

'A machine passed over a little while ago. I thought it was you, but it went right on.'

'How are you going to get these papers from Zorlan?' asked Ginger.

'Ask him for them. It's no use mincing words at this stage.'

'And if he refuses to hand them over?'

'I shall take them.'

'If I'm any judge he'll cut up rough.'

'He can cut up as rough as he likes. When I tell him the game's up, if he's wise he'll pack it in. What else can he do? Fight the lot of us? Damage the plane and get himself stuck here? Don't worry. Whatever he tries on we should be able to handle it. I'm taking those papers home. That's definite.'

'Here he comes now, complete with portfolio,' resumed Bertie. 'He must be wondering what all this nattering is about.'

'Okay. Stand by for trouble if that's how he wants it.'

'What if he pulls a gun?'

'I've got one. So have you.'

Zorlan came up. 'What's the news?' he inquired, looking from one to the other. His eyes came to rest on Biggles.

'The news, Professor Zorlan, is this. I must ask you to hand over that portfolio.'

It was evident this demand came as a shock. Zorlan took a pace back. 'I shall do nothing of the sort.'

'If you won't give it to me I shall have to take it.'

'What right have you to talk like this to me?'

'I have received fresh orders from London. I am now in charge of the operation.'

'So that's where the plane has been,' sneered Zorlan.

'No matter where it's been, it's been far enough. You don't need me to go into details, but your scheme is known and it's all washed up. I'm putting the matter to you fairly and squarely in the hope you'll have the good sense not to make a fuss.'

'This portfolio is my personal property and neither you nor anyone else has any right to touch it!' exclaimed Zorlan with a show of indignation.

Biggles went on dispassionately. 'The case may be yours, but the papers in it are not. You can have the case back when I've taken out certain papers it contains.'

Zorlan's face had turned pale. That was something beyond his control. The same with the malice in his eyes. 'What do you expect to find?'

'That sort of bluff won't help you. In particular I want the document the sheikh refused to sign, the one that would have given you an outrageous share in his oil profits.'

'Ah! So he told you.'

'Of course he did. He's not a fool. He has every right
to safeguard his interests. He asked me to check with
London and I have done so. You know as well as I do,
now, that you had no right to ask the sheikh to put his
name to any document other than those that were given
to you to present to him.'

'What are you going to do with it?'

'Burn it. It's no use to you, anyhow. The sheikh won't
sign it. I shall tell him not to.'

Zorlan's usually imperturbable face was a picture of
hate and chagrin.

Biggles put out a hand. 'The case, please.'

Zorlan took another pace back. He whipped out an
automatic. 'Try to take it from me at your peril,' he
grated.

Biggles shook his head sadly. 'I thought you were an
intelligent man, but now you're behaving like a fool.
What do you hope to gain by this nonsense? You can't
get away from here. When the sheikh comes, and he
should be here any minute now, and I tell him the facts,
it's likely that he will have something to say. You may
find him less tolerant than I am trying to be – particularly if I mention you had the lunatic idea of seizing
his fiancée as a hostage. Use your head and save yourself
worse trouble. Give me that case and I'll undertake to fly
you back to London or, if you wish, drop you off at any
intermediate airport on the way.'

As he finished Biggles stepped forward and took the
portfolio from Zorlan's hand. Zorlan did not resist.
You can put that pistol away,' advised Biggles.

The case was locked.

Again Biggles put out a hand. 'The key, please.'

Zorlan handed it over.

Biggles unlocked the case, ran through the documents until he found the one he wanted. He passed it to Bertie. 'Put a match to that.'

Bertie held it up and set fire to one corner. Nobody moved or spoke while the flame consumed it. The black ash dropped to the ground.

'Now you've got what you wanted you will let me have the rest of the papers,' said Zorlan sourly.

'Certainly not.'

'Why not?'

'As you no longer enjoy the confidence of my government, my orders are to hold them in safe custody until I can return them to London.' Biggles handed back the empty portfolio. The packet of papers, too bulky to go into his pocket, he gave to Bertie. 'Put those in a safe place in the machine.'

Zorlan again looked from one to the other. He found no sympathy. 'Very well,' he said icily. 'But let me tell you something. This isn't the end.'

'It is as far as I'm concerned.'

'That's what you may think.'

'Any more of that sort of talk and I shall think twice about taking you home,' promised Biggles sternly. 'You're not quite out of the wood yourself, if it comes to that.'

Zorlan turned abruptly and strode away.

'Take his gun,' urged Ginger.

Biggles shrugged. 'We've done enough. Let him go and think it over.' He looked up at the sky, now turning egg-shell blue with the near approach of day. 'I'll take a walk up the hill to see if there's any sign of the sheikh. I shall be more than ever glad to see the end of this disagreeable business.'

'Hark!' said Ginger.

Biggles, who was walking away, stopped. 'Damnation take it,' he muttered savagely.

From a long way off came the unmistakable growl of aero engines.

CHAPTER 12

THE BATTLE OF QUARDA

For perhaps ten seconds no one spoke. They all stood rigid, listening intently.

'It's coming this way,' said Ginger.

'It isn't a MIG,' stated Bertie.

'Whatever it is it's coming from the east, which means it'll be no friend of ours,' prophesied Biggles. 'It may be that machine I heard come over half an hour ago, going home. Let's have a look.'

They hurried round the base of the hill to a spot where the view eastward was not interrupted by trees or the rising ground.

'There it is,' observed Biggles, coming to a halt. 'A four engined job.'

'It's dead on course for us,' said Bertie.

'Yes, and I don't like it. That's a military type. What's it doing here? I smell mischief.'

'What are we going to do?'

'What *can* we do?'

'We could chuck some camouflage over the Merlin,' suggested Ginger.

'Hold hard a minute,' returned Biggles. 'Before we

get in a flap we'd better wait to see if this is the objective. It's holding its altitude, so it might be going right over. If it intended coming down here it would be losing height by now.'

'Machine guns won't do much damage from where it is,' declared Ginger optimistically.

'That doesn't mean it may not use heavier stuff.'

'Bombs?'

'Could be.' Biggles' eyes were still on the approaching aircraft. 'It looks mighty like a bomber type.' He lowered his eyes to scan the desert. 'Where the devil's the sheikh? He should have been here before this.'

'What difference would he make?' inquired Ginger.

'A lot. If he were here I'd feel inclined to make a run for it. I'm pretty sure we could show our tail to that lumbering crate. But it's no use talking about that. The sheikh said he'd be coming here, so we can count on it. We can't just push off and leave him. Besides, there's the girl. She complicates matters. We can't bolt and leave her here. If we did that and anything happened to her we'd be called some ugly names. If we took her with us and things went wrong it'd come to the same thing. We'd be blamed for putting her in the machine.'

'If anything does start she'll be in just as much danger here,' Ginger pointed out practically. 'That palm-frond shelter she's in wouldn't be any protection.'

'You're right. It wouldn't.'

Bertie spoke. 'Well, what are we going to do? If we're going to do anything it's time we were getting on with it. I'm all against sitting here in the middle of what may presently be a target area.'

Biggles made up his mind suddenly. 'Let's get back to the machine for a start. Whatever happens we must save

it or we're likely to be here for keeps. Those papers are
in it and they're precious. Where did you put 'em,
Bertie?'

'Under the seat where we hid the pistols.'

By this time they were hurrying back to the camp.
With the unknown machine nearly overhead it could be
seen from almost any position.

Biggles spoke tersely. 'Listen, Ginger. You get in the
cockpit, start up and be ready to move fast. Just keep
ticking over so as not to raise a dust.'

'What's the idea?'

'If there's trouble I shall put the girl in the cabin with
one of the guards and you'll make a dash for Suwara. If
you don't meet the sheikh on the way you may find him
there. Hand the girl over to him. If there are no MIGs
about you can come back here and have a look at the
place. If you can't see us head for home with those
papers. Don't on any account land unless you get an
okay signal from me. If everything is all right I'll show
myself in the open.'

'I get it.'

Bertie stepped in. 'But look here, old boy; without
knowing their language, how are you going to tell the
guards what you're going to do? I mean to say, if you try
touching that lass you're liable to get a scimitar in the
neck.'

'Zorlan can explain. Where the devil is he?' Biggles
looked around. The guards stood on duty, but Zorlan
was not to be seen. 'Zorlan!' he shouted. 'Zorlan! Where
are you? Come here.'

There was no answer. The man did not appear.

'Confound the fellow. What's he up to?' raged
Biggles.

By this time the air was filled with the roar of aero engines overhead.

'You get started up,' Biggles told Ginger brusquely. 'Watch me for a signal. Don't move until you get one. I shall have to try to make the guards understand.'

'Okay.' Ginger ran to the machine.

Biggles strode to where the guards were standing in a group by the palm-shelter calmly watching what was going on. Reaching them, he used his hands in an effort to explain what he wanted, first pointing up, then at the shelter, then at the Merlin. He thought the urgency with which he did this would be enough to make them understand that danger threatened; but each man merely looked at the others as if seeking inspiration.

Still struggling with the problem, he heard the Merlin's engines spring to life. A moment later this was followed by a wild yell from Bertie. He was pointing up. Biggles' eyes followed the direction and what he saw settled any doubts he had had about touching the girl.

Dropping from the aircraft were not the bombs he half expected, but a line of men on parachutes. Seven or eight were on their way down. He didn't wait to see how many there were altogether. For a second he hesitated. So that was why the big machine had held its altitude! Naturally, his first thought was to bundle everyone in the Merlin and run for it, confident that the troop-carrier would not be able to catch him. Then he remembered the sheikh. By this time he would be well on his way to the ruins. When he arrived he would ride straight into the hands of the enemies. Or so Biggles could only assume. He had no idea who the parachutists were, but they could hardly be friends of the sheikh. He shouted again for Zorlan, but there was no response.

He could wait no longer. Grabbing a guard by the arm, he pointed at what was dropping from the sky. Surely, he thought, the man would understand *that*. He pulled him towards the shelter making signs by pointing at the Merlin and repeating 'Suwara – Suwara.'

The problem was more or less solved for him when the girl herself appeared, pushing aside the fronds that covered the entrance to the shelter. She was still veiled, but he caught a glimpse of a pair of dark, startled eyes, through a two-inch slit in the head covering. He beckoned desperately, stabbing a finger towards the aircraft. To his great relief she appeared to understand, for she walked towards it. The guards followed in a group, but Biggles held them back except one.

They reached the machine. Bertie had opened the door. The girl took her seat. The selected guard got in with her. Biggles touched his rifle, a modern weapon, and bandolier, making pantomime gestures that he needed them to shoot at the parachutists. The man looked doubtful but handed the things over. Biggles slammed the door and fastened it on the inside. He went through to the cockpit to Ginger.

'Okay. Get weaving. Dump the passengers at Suwara. Never mind about us. If you come back and can't see us press on regardless for home and hand those papers to the chief.'

'Right.'

Biggles jumped down, waved a hand and the Merlin sped away across the wilderness. He watched it until it was clear and then, satisfied that the pilot of the unknown aircraft hadn't noticed it, or if he had he had chosen to ignore it, he turned to find Bertie waiting. The four remaining guards were standing by him. They, understandably, were looking perplexed, although Biggles had no doubt they would grasp the situation when the shooting started.

'Seen Zorlan?' he asked laconically.

'No.'

'What's he up to? He must have seen what was happening.'

'Taken cover or gone into hiding somewhere, I imagine.'

'Could you see how many men were dropped?'

'I counted twelve.'

'Let's try to find out what they're doing. Keep your head down. We don't want them to see us.' Biggles walked quickly up the slope to a vantage point and dropped behind some crumbling stumps of stone-masonry that had once been the wall of a house.

The unknown aircraft was now droning overhead in wide circles. The parachutists had of course landed over a fairly large area of the open ground rather than risk injury on the ruin-strewn hill. Discarding their parachutes, they were converging in open order towards the rising ground under the direction of a man who obviously was the leader. They wore dun-coloured battle-dress and with two exceptions were armed with what looked like ordinary service rifles. The other two carried light machine guns. Their faces gave no indication of their nationality. They were dark, but in the Middle East or Western Asia they might have been called white. They were something less than a hundred yards away.

'What do you make of 'em?' asked Bertie.

'I haven't a clue. If that machine's carrying nationality marks I can't see them.'

'What's the drill?'

'We could pick some of 'em off now, while they're in the open. It'll be more difficult when they get under cover.'

'Then why not give 'em a rattle?'

Biggles frowned. 'I don't like opening fire on men who may turn out to be – well, if not friends, not enemies. That would be the quickest way to make them enemies.'

'If we let 'em get too close we've had it.'

'I'll fire a shot over their heads to see what effect that has.' Biggles did so.

This told them all they wanted to know, for the effect of the shot was to produce a burst of machine-gun fire, the bullets spattering all over the place, as was to be expected since the man carrying the weapon had not stopped to take proper aim.

This in turn had an effect Biggles had not anticipated. The guards, who had lain down behind the same wall, did not wait for orders. This was something they understood and they did not wait for a second invitation from the enemy to take part in the proceedings. They opened a ragged fire; but apparently they knew how to shoot for three men fell in quick succession. The others broke into a run, swerving away towards a different part of the hill.

'That's done it,' said Biggles grimly. 'Well, having started, we might as well carry on.' He fired, and another man stumbled into the sand.

'That's thinned 'em out a bit,' observed Bertie. 'Eight left.'

'That's plenty for us to hold off. Keep your gun for close work.'

The guards were still shooting. Another man fell.

'Seven,' said Bertie.

'It'll be a different matter when they get into cover,' predicted Biggles. 'It'll be a stalking and sniping proposition.'

Then an extraordinary thing happened. To Biggles, and no doubt to Bertie, it was so unexpected that for a moment neither spoke. With the enemy not more than thirty yards from the hill and the cover they needed, out of a group of palms ran a figure waving a white flag – or to be more correct, a handkerchief tied to the end of a stick.

'That's Zorlan,' gasped Biggles. 'What the hell does he think he's doing?'

'He's decided to change sides, that's all,' sneered Bertie.

Zorlan did not get far. Whether the attackers did not understand the western meaning of a white flag, or perhaps suspected a trick, was a matter for conjecture. There was of course the possibility that they had been ordered not to take prisoners. Be that as it may, shots were fired. Zorlan crumpled and rolled over and over to the bottom of the hill. He did not move again.

'Serves him right for ratting on us,' observed Bertie without emotion. 'He reckoned to be on the winning side to get his own back.'

A few more shots were fired just before the attacking force reached cover and disappeared from sight.

'D'you know something?' queried Bertie in a curious voice.

'Tell me.'

'Just before he disappeared I had a good look at the chap who seemed to be in charge. I had a second look because he was the first to fire at Zorlan. If I haven't seen him before I'll swallow my eyeglass. He's changed his togs since I last saw him.'

'Who do you think he was?'

'Alfondari. The man was his build and walked like him. Moreover, his face wasn't as dark as the rest of 'em.'

Biggles whistled softly. 'Well, I suppose that would be possible. He was always on the other side. I don't see how it can make any difference – except that he has a personal grudge against us. He'd no time for Zorlan, either. We know that. But never mind him. This is where the serious business starts. Let's get into a better position, facing them.'

This was done, the guards going with them. Far from looking alarmed, they appeared to be enjoying themselves. Probably used to tribal warfare, this was obviously a game they had played before.

The unidentified aircraft had now come down and landed on the open ground nearly half a mile away, presumably to be out of range of the defenders, yet ready to pick up the paratroops when they had finished their work. The engines were switched off. To Biggles' relief it did not unload reinforcements for the men already on the ground.

Silence fell, a brittle, attentive silence.

'Are we going to winkle 'em out?' asked Bertie.

'Not likely. Let them come for us.'

Five minutes passed. Nothing happened. There came no sound to indicate where the attackers were or in which direction they had gone. Biggles, knowing the folly of impatience in such circumstances, did not move a muscle. Nor did Bertie. But it seemed that one of the guards, who should have known better, did not share

this view. Before Biggles could stop him he moved to
what apparently he thought was a better position, and as
if that was not taking enough risk he peeped over the
parapet formed by the broken wall. Tragedy came like a
flash of lightning. A rifle cracked. He collapsed and slid
down the slight slope to end up face downwards almost
at Biggles' feet. Biggles turned him over. There was a
little hole in the centre of his forehead. There was no
need to say anything. The faces of his companions were
inscrutable.

Bertie picked up the dead man's rifle, and removing
one of his bandoliers, slung it over his shoulder. He
opened the breech to make sure there was a cartridge in
the chamber.

For half an hour, a taut, nerve-straining period, the
scene remained unchanged. Once Biggles dragged himself a little way to get a view of the wilderness, hoping to
see the sheikh coming with a strong escort; but there was
not a movement. The only object to catch the eye was
the dark-painted plane standing at a safe distance. He
wormed his way back to Bertie. 'No use looking for help
from the sheikh,' he breathed. 'He isn't even in sight. If
he appeared now, riding tired horses, the party would be
some time getting here.'

Bertie did not answer. He merely grimaced to show
that he had heard. Rifle to shoulder, only his eyes moved
as he continued to scrutinise the ruins and other possible
cover around them – wind-blown palms, camel-thorn,
and the like. There might not have been a living creature
within miles for any sound that came to prove otherwise; yet it would have been stupid to suppose the
enemy was sitting still. It would be something to know
from which direction they were approaching. Finding

the strain intolerable, he inched his way to Biggles and suggested that he made a reconnaissance.

Biggles would not consider it. 'Wait,' he whispered. 'They'll come.'

The three remaining natives were watching, too, their dark eyes alert. They lay like logs.

The day wore on. The heat as the sun climbed over its zenith became a torment, dehydrating the body to leave the mouth and lips parched. There were some bottles of soda water down at the camp. In the rush of events they had been left there. The temptation to fetch one or two was not easy to resist, but convinced the enemy could not be far away, Biggles did not succumb. Even to move to a new position out of the sun would probably be fatal. The enemy might be waiting for just that.

The end, when it came, was sudden.

Machine guns chattered and bullets raked the broken wall, sending sand and fragments of masonry flying. The shooting ended abruptly, to be followed instantly by shouts as the enemy sprang up and charged from so short a distance that Biggles was shocked that they had been able to get so close. They were met with a volley that was more hasty than accurate. One at least fell. The guards, in their enthusiasm to get to grips at last, dashed forward, also yelling, shooting indiscriminately, or so it seemed to Biggles, who had to hold his fire for fear of hitting his own men. The result was inevitable. Two of the guards went down, although one continued shooting. The other dodged behind some stonework from where he kept up a rapid fire. The enemy, not liking this, dived for cover, and the charge ended as quickly as it had begun. The shooting stopped. How many of the enemy had been hit Biggles did not know. What upset him was the loss of two men, leaving only one of the guards on his feet; and just where he had gone he was by no means sure.

He turned to see Bertie holding a bloodstained handkerchief to his face.

'Only a splinter – bit of stone or something,' explained Bertie in answer to Biggles' expression of alarm. He went flat as another burst of machine-gun fire sprayed the ground in front to kick more debris into the air.

Biggles tied the handkerchief over what turned out to be a nasty cut on Bertie's cheek. He was looking grave, for it was evident the enemy knew exactly where they were and with only three of them left – assuming the one remaining guard was still alive – the end could not be far off. Nothing could be done. They couldn't face machine-gun fire with any hope of survival and to retire down the hill behind them would gain no advantage. The enemy would follow and eventually drive them on to the open ground.

Minutes passed.

Then through the lull came a sound. It was the hum of an aircraft, rising as it came nearer. Biggles wriggled a yard or two until he could see it. 'It's Ginger,' he told Bertie grimly. 'He's flying low. I hope to heaven he isn't thinking of landing. I told him to keep clear unless I made a signal.'

'He won't land,' declared Bertie confidently. 'He's bound to see that machine standing in the open.'

'Then why is he losing height?'

'Maybe he just wants to have a look round.'

'He must be crazy to risk coming so low. It's those papers I'm thinking about. If they're lost the whole stinking business will have been a waste of time.'

The Merlin, still losing height on half throttle, made a tight circuit of the hill. Then, with engines idling, it began what was clearly an approach run towards the usual landing ground.

'He's coming down,' fumed Biggles. 'Cover me as far as you can.'

Jumping to his feet, he raced down the hill.

CHAPTER 13

HOW IT ALL ENDED

By the time Biggles had reached the bottom of the hill the Merlin was on the ground, taxiing tail up towards the camp. He ran towards it waving his arms in desperate signals, hoping Ginger would interpret them correctly and take off again. The aircraft came on regardless. Reaching the camp site it swung round, its tail cutting a circle in the sand, to bring the cabin door into view. The engines died with a gasp as they were switched off. The cockpit exit was opened and Ginger jumped down.

Biggles, white with anger, strode towards him; but what he intended to say was never spoken, which may have been just as well, for the cabin door was now pushed open and out came the sheikh, rifle in hand, closely followed by six men, also armed.

Unprepared for this, Biggles came to a skidding halt. All he could think to say was: 'Didn't you see that enemy plane standing there?'

'Of course I saw it,' answered Ginger calmly. 'The sheikh ordered me down. He wanted to come here. He thought you might need help.'

'You're dead right, we do; the men the sheikh left with us are all dead, except one, and he may be a gonner by now for all I know.'

The sheikh must have overheard this, for he said: 'So these enemy troops are still here?'

'They are.'

'How many?'

'I'm not sure. About six or seven. We got some of them. On our side we're down to three all told. We were still fighting it out when you arrived. You know how this started?'

'I travelled beside your young friend in the cockpit and he told me.'

'Is Bertie all right?' put in Ginger anxiously.

'He was when I left him. Not knowing who you had on board, I came down to tell you to clear off.'

'I don't think that will be necessary,' said the sheikh quietly. He spoke to his men in their own language and with rifles at the ready they streamed off up the hill. 'They will deal with any further trouble,' he added with a smile.

Biggles fetched a bottle of soda water and poured the contents down his throat. 'Phew!' he panted. 'It was almost worth being roasted for that. I must take a bottle up to Bertie.'

'I would say he'll be down any minute now,' said the sheikh, as firing broke out on the hill. He walked a little way towards it.

'In that case I'll wait a bit.' Biggles looked back at Ginger. 'How did this come about?'

'As you'd expect. I was making for Suwara when I met the sheikh heading this way. At least, I saw a party of horsemen heading for here and couldn't imagine it would be anyone else. I went low to make sure; then I landed and told him how matters stood.'

'You mentioned who was in the cabin?'

'Of course. He agreed you'd done the right thing. He asked me to fly her on to Suwara. He came with us. That's why I've been so long. He had to give some orders. Then he collected the troops and – well, here we are.'

'What about the original party of horsemen he had with him in the desert?'

'They kept straight on for here. Six of 'em. They must be getting close.'

The sheikh came back. 'I'm sorry to have kept you waiting so long. As I told you, I hoped to get back soon after dawn, but I found I had several things to do.'

'Maybe it was well you didn't get back earlier,' returned Biggles. 'For a while the position looked pretty black.'

'All the more reason why I should have been here.'

'That's what I'd expect you to say. By the way, sir, you'll be interested to know that Zorlan is dead. At least, I think he is. It was impossible to get near him to make sure.'

'How did that happen?'

'It was his own fault. He ran towards the enemy waving a white flag, so we can only suppose he had decided to surrender or go over to the enemy. He didn't get a chance to explain. They shot him. He fell in the open, so there was nothing we could do about it.'

'A strange man,' murmured the sheikh. 'I wonder what he hoped to gain by turning traitor or playing the coward. It must have been one or the other. I was told by your young friend here that you had taken the contracts away from him on receiving orders from London to do so. I'm infinitely grateful to you —' he broke off as shooting, more distant now, broke out.

Bertie, taking long strides, came down the hill. 'It's all over,' he announced. 'They're running to their plane. A party of horsemen has just rolled up and they're pooping off at it. There go the engines. Give me a drink someone before I perish of thirst.'

As Ginger ran to fetch a bottle the engines of the unknown aircraft roared as it took off.

'I'm glad it has got away,' said the sheikh. 'Had it been destroyed here it would have been difficult to explain. It might have provided an excuse for war.'

'It'll go home with fewer men than it came out with,' Biggles pointed out.

'I shall know nothing whatever about that,' answered the sheikh calmly.

'In that case it might be a good thing to see about clearing up. There's quite a bit to be done.'

'That needn't worry you. My men will attend to it.'

'That being so, may I assume it will be all right for us to return home? The sooner I can hand over these documents to my chief the happier I shall be.'

'Do you mean you want to go now, immediately?'

'As soon as I've had a wash, shave, and a brush up. At the moment I'm not exactly feeling my best and brightest.'

The sheikh smiled. 'Then why not come to my house and take a bath? I'm thinking of myself, too. I would like to get home as soon as possible. If you would be kind enough to fly me there it would save a lot of time.'

Biggles looked at the others. Ginger winked. 'I call that a clinking idea,' said Bertie. 'I'm all for it. Wash some of the sand off the old body, if you see what I mean. It's beginning to tickle.'

Biggles turned back to the sheikh. 'We shall be very happy to accept your invitation, sir. But if I may say so without discourtesy, we must not stay long. As there may still be hostile aircraft about, I would prefer to travel after dark, taking our leave when the moon is up.'

'I quite understand.'

'To come back to the present,' went on Biggles. 'What about your men here? I refer particularly to those who flew out with you. As they have no horses, do you want me to take them back?'

'No. There is plenty for them to do here. They will be some time. When I get home I will send a relief party out with spare horses, food and other things that will be required. But I would like you to take back any of my men who are wounded.'

'As you wish.'

At this juncture three men came down the hill carrying a body, no doubt because it wore European clothes. They put it on the ground in the shade of some palms. It was, of course, Professor Zorlan. Biggles walked over.

He looked down and shook his head sadly. 'What a pity he had to throw away his life as he did,' he murmured. 'I'm sure he had his good points. What comes over men?'

'The passion for wealth makes some people mad.' said the sheikh philosophically. 'Are you going to take the body home?'

Biggles shook his head. 'That might lead to awkward questions at any intermediate airport where I may land. There doesn't seem any point in it. No, I shall leave him here and he can be buried with the rest.'

Other bodies were brought down. Biggles glanced at them. 'If that was Alfondari you saw,' he told Bertie, 'he seems to have got away with it.'

One of the sheikh's men had been wounded. After being given preliminary treatment, he was made comfortable in the cabin.

'If that's all, I think we'd be wise to move off while things are quiet,' suggested Biggles.

The sheikh agreed.

There is no need to dwell on the lavish hospitality the airmen received at the sheikh's palace, a strong guard having been put on the Merlin. Feeling considerably better for a luxurious toilet and a substantial meal, they stayed on talking over the recent events until the moon was high in the sky, when Biggles said it was time they were going. As a matter of detail, one of the things discussed was the formation of a small Zarat Air Force, for desert patrols, which the sheikh thought might be made financially possible by his oil revenues, when they were forthcoming. Would Biggles prepare a modest scheme, on paper in the first instance, but with more practical help later on?

Biggles said he would think it over, pointing out that as a government employee he was not a free agent in such matters.

In accordance with local custom, the girl who had been a passenger in the aircraft was not mentioned. They never saw her again; so whether she was young and beautiful, or old and plain, had to remain a matter for speculation.

At the end they parted on the most cordial terms, with a standing invitation to make the palace their home at any time.

Biggles then set a course for Athens, having decided that should be their first and only stop.

The following evening he handed the all-important documents to the Air Commodore. As will be imagined, he had a lot of explaining to do; but there is no need to go into what would be mostly repetition.